The next ten minutes were filled with talk of the weekend. Once or twice Amy tried to make a comment, but no one really seemed to notice. *What's going on here?* she wondered. Usually, Amy was the center of attention. Now, nobody even noticed she was alive.

It would be different if I had a boyfriend, she thought fiercely, sneaking an envious glance at Elizabeth and Todd. *It's obvious I can't rely on my friends.* Elizabeth and Todd were so happy together. Todd seemed to anticipate everything Elizabeth needed.

That was what Amy wanted. Someone to cuddle up with at football games, someone to take long walks with on the beach. No more flirting and chasing and pursuing and getting herself in weird situations. She wanted something steady, something *serious*. Someone who would love her for who she was.

Amy turned away. *Just wait,* she vowed. *They won't treat me this way once I've gotten things off the ground with Tom McKay!*

Bantam Books in the Sweet Valley High Series
Ask your bookseller for the books you have missed

SWEET VALLEY HIGH

AMY'S TRUE LOVE

Written by
Kate William

Created by
FRANCINE PASCAL

BANTAM BOOKS
NEW YORK · TORONTO · LONDON · SYDNEY · AUCKLAND

RL 6, age 12 and up

AMY'S TRUE LOVE
A Bantam Book / May 1991

Sweet Valley High is a registered trademark of Francine Pascal

Conceived by Francine Pascal

Produced by Daniel Weiss Associates, Inc.
33 West 17th Street
New York, NY 10011

Cover art by James Mathewuse

ISBN 0-553-28963-2

Published simultaneously in the United States and Canada

Bantam Books are published by Bantam Books, a division of Bantam Doubleday Dell Publishing Group, Inc. Its trademark, consisting of the words "Bantam Books" and the portrayal of a rooster, is Registered in U.S. Patent and Trademark Office and in other countries. Marca Registrada. Bantam Books, 666 Fifth Avenue, New York, New York 10103.

PRINTED IN THE UNITED STATES OF AMERICA

OPM   0 9 8 7 6 5 4 3 2 1

AMY'S TRUE LOVE

One

"I don't understand it," Jessica Wakefield declared, picking up a "Mystery Sandwich" and dropping it on her tray. "Why do school lunches have to look like something from *The Twilight Zone*?"

Her twin sister Elizabeth laughed and reached for a carton of yogurt and an apple. "I thought you were on a liquid diet this week," she said, pushing her tray up to the cash register and taking out her wallet.

Jessica tossed back her silken blond hair. "I changed my mind. I decided it isn't healthy. Although," she added with a grimace, studying her sandwich, "who knows whether this is any better?"

Elizabeth picked up her tray and surveyed the crowded cafeteria. Lunchtime at Sweet Valley High was always lively and today was no

1

exception. "We may have to eat standing up," Elizabeth said ruefully.

Jessica's eyes flicked expertly over the crowded tables. "It's all Amy Sutton's fault," she grumbled. "She was supposed to meet me twenty minutes ago, and she never showed up. If I hadn't had to wait for her, I could've gotten any seat I wanted."

"I take it that means you weren't planning on eating lunch with your twin sister after all," Elizabeth said dryly. "I just happened to be the only available second choice!"

"Oh, you know what I mean," Jessica said evasively. "But seriously, Liz, Amy's really flaking out lately," she continued as the girls steered their way to two empty seats. Jessica set her tray down. Her pretty face was flushed with irritation. "She's been really unreliable. And she's always late to everything. She's so inconsiderate!"

Elizabeth hid a smile. Look who was complaining about someone being late! Elizabeth had spent far too many hours of her sixteen years waiting for her twin, who never wore a watch and ran on what Elizabeth jokingly called JST—Jessica Standard Time.

"Maybe Amy got delayed by something important," Elizabeth said as she opened her carton of yogurt.

Jessica rolled her eyes. "Yeah. She's probably hitting on some guy. And that's another thing. You know how boy-crazy Amy is, right? Well, even I have to admit that lately she's beginning to go a bit overboard. *All* she talks about anymore is guys. She's dying for a boyfriend, and

2

every guy she sees becomes a likely target!" Jessica shook her head. "I mean, I still really like Amy, but she's driving me *crazy*."

Elizabeth looked thoughtfully at her sister. For once it sounded as if she and Jessica were on the same wavelength. More often than not, the twins' thoughts were as divergent as east and west, belying their mirror-perfect resemblance to each other. Sometimes Elizabeth joked to Todd Wilkins, her long-time steady boyfriend, that they really *were* like mirror images—identical in one way and opposite in another!

People who did not know the twins well often got them confused. Their older brother Steven, who was a freshman at the nearby state university, called his sisters the "clones." Both girls were a slender size six. Both had long blond hair, eyes the blue-green of the Pacific Ocean, and each showed a tiny dimple in her left cheek when she smiled. The girls even wore matching lavaliere necklaces, presents from their parents on their sixteenth birthday.

But that was where their similarities ended. Elizabeth was hard-working, loyal, and responsible. She devoted a lot of her free time to writing for *The Oracle*, the school newspaper. And when she wanted to relax and have fun, she would spend time with her steady boyfriend, Todd Wilkins, or her best friend, Enid Rollins.

Jessica loved excitement and change and being in the thick of things. She threw herself into every new relationship and situation with characteristic energy and abandon. Jessica just could not understand how her sister could sit and read a novel when there was so much else to do. She herself would much rather practice some cheers or hang out with her large group of friends than read or spend time with only one boy.

Amy Sutton was one of Jessica's closest friends. Ironically, Amy had been one of Elizabeth's best friends ever since Sweet Valley Elementary School. But when Amy's family had moved away, the girls' friendship had naturally lapsed. Then, earlier in their junior year, Amy's family had moved back to Sweet Valley so Mrs. Sutton could take a job as a sportscaster on a local television station. Elizabeth was thrilled at the news. But the new Amy Sutton was nothing like the sixth-grader Elizabeth had known. The new Amy liked clothes, makeup, and *boys*! While Elizabeth had found the new Amy not at all her type, Jessica had taken up with her immediately. It amused Elizabeth now to hear Jessica claim Amy was suddenly boy-crazy.

"She can't be any more boy-crazy than she's been all year," Elizabeth objected.

"Oh, but she is," Jessica said vehemently. "Listen to this. She and I were at the Beach Disco on Saturday night, and there was this incredibly cute guy there, Dan somebody. I never got to find out his last name, because Amy was all over him. You should have heard her!" Jessica pursed her lips in imitation of her friend. " 'Dan! Why, that's my favorite name!' Ugh!" She shuddered at the memory.

Elizabeth took a spoonful of yogurt. "Uh-oh.

4

Sounds like somebody's stepping on your turf, Jess."

Jessica ignored her sister's comment. "She's totally out of control. Standing me up for lunch is really too much." She shrugged. "Well, I guess that's why they say blood is thicker than water, Liz. When your friends abandon you, you can still count on your sister to have lunch with you."

"Thanks, Jess," Elizabeth said, rolling her eyes. "You really know how to flatter me."

"Look! There's Cara and Lila and Jean," Jessica said, getting up so fast she knocked over her milk carton. "Sorry, Liz, I've got to go talk to them." Her aquamarine eyes twinkled as she focused on Jean West. "I've been hearing rumors all morning long that Jeanie and Tom McKay are splitting up. You don't mind if I find out the truth for myself, do you?"

"Go ahead," Elizabeth reassured her twin. "I've got to meet Todd soon anyway. He's waiting for me in the library." She pulled her hair back with one hand. "I can't believe Jean and Tom are splitting up. They seemed like a terrific couple."

"Well, that's what Sandra Bacon told me. And she should know. She and Jean are like this," Jessica said, holding two of her fingers up close together.

Elizabeth watched her twin sister bound off toward her friends. A glance at her watch told her that her lunch with Jessica had been even shorter than she had expected. Well, she had

5

gotten ten minutes of Jessica's time with no interruptions! That was something of a record.

Jean West was surrounded by sympathetic friends. Cara Walker sat on her left, Lila Fowler on her right, and Sandra Bacon across from her, next to Jessica.

Jean was a member of the cheerleading squad along with Cara, Sandra, and Jessica. She was a striking girl, petite and quiet, with long dark hair and beautiful green eyes. But her eyes were filled with pain as she confided to her closest friends what had happened with Tom McKay.

"It's over, you guys. Really over," she said mournfully. "I've known for a while the end was coming. We reached the point where we just couldn't kid ourselves anymore."

"But I don't understand. I thought you two were the perfect couple," Cara said sadly.

Jean shook her head. "I thought so, too," she admitted. "I keep thinking about how it all started as a dare, and then turned into something really special. Now it's all over."

Jessica remembered when Jean had asked Tom out as part of her pledge for Pi Beta Alpha. After all, as president of the elite sorority, she had been involved in the whole incident. But it quickly became obvious that Jean really liked Tom and it seemed that Tom liked her as well.

Jean put her elbows on the table and rested her head in her hands. "I don't know what happened. We used to spend all our free time together. But then Tom started spending more

6

time playing tennis." Jean was almost oblivious to her friends who were hanging on her every word. "It's not that I was jealous of the time he spent practicing," she continued. "It was just that even when we were together, it was as if we were buddies, not boyfriend and girlfriend."

Lila shook her head. As the only daughter of one of the wealthiest men in the entire state, Lila often presumed she knew the best way to do everything. "Sounds like the romance fizzled, Jean. Maybe you two just need, you know, a little more *quality* time." She looked at Jean knowingly. "A little more time up at Miller's Point, for instance."

Jean blushed. Miller's Point was a popular parking spot overlooking the valley. "Let's put it this way, Lila. That side of things, well, you're right. The romance *did* fizzle. But I don't think an hour at Miller's Point is going to change anything. It's over, and I think the sooner I accept that, the better." Her green eyes were filled with sadness. "I love Tom, as a friend. And that's all we can be for now."

The whole table was quiet as the girls looked sympathetically at Jean. "Poor thing," Sandra whispered, putting her hand over her friend's.

"If there's anything any of us can do . . ." Cara added softly.

"Seriously, Jean. We're your friends and we're here to help you," Lila said grandly.

Jean wiped a tear from her eye. "The worst thing was that Tom was so relieved when I suggested breaking up! I half thought, half hoped, he'd say no. But he looked . . ." Jean's voice

7

faltered a little, "so grateful. . . ." She choked back tears. "He was as upset as I was that our relationship wasn't working out. He said it had been bothering him, but that he had been too scared to bring it up himself."

Sandra squeezed Jean's hand. "Don't hold back. Go ahead and cry," she urged.

Jean pulled her hand away and wiped savagely at her eyes. "No, I'm fine." She took a deep breath. "Hey, move over a little, Li. Here comes Amy."

Jessica turned. Sure enough, Amy was bouncing along, tray in hand, looking totally unconcerned. She had obviously completely forgotten her lunch date with Jessica.

"Jean West," Amy said, setting her tray down on the table without a word of greeting for anyone else. "I am in a *complete* state of shock! I just ran into Maria Santelli, and she told me that you and Tom are history!"

Lila gave Amy a warning look, which Amy did not heed.

"I couldn't believe my ears!" Amy pulled up a chair and opened her carton of chocolate milk. "And she also said *you* were the one who did the breaking up. Are you out of your mind? Don't you realize Tom McKay's one of the cutest guys in the whole school!"

Jean opened her mouth, shook her head, but could not say a word.

"Amy, take it easy," Cara advised.

"Well, if *she's* the one who broke up with *him*, why all the sad faces? This looks like a

8

funeral party!" Amy cried, popping a french fry into her mouth.

Cara cleared her throat. "Maybe we should change the subject," she said meaningfully. "Did I tell you guys what happened to me this morning in Spanish class? I—"

Amy worked her way through the french fries with furious speed. Her gray eyes fixed thoughtfully on Jean. "I don't want to be tacky or anything, Jean," she interrupted, "but the truth is, I've always had a little bit of a crush on Tom. In fact, I've had my eye on him for weeks now. Now that you've broken up with him, you wouldn't mind if I tried to get to know him a little better, would you?"

Jean turned pale. "I've got to go now," Jean said suddenly. She pushed back her chair and got to her feet.

"I'll come with you," Sandra said quickly.

"Wow!" Amy grabbed a few more fries as Jean fled and Sandra hurried after her. "Welcome to soap-opera city! She sure seems to be taking it hard. Why did she break up with him if she still cares so much?"

Jessica couldn't control herself any longer. "Amy, can't you show even an ounce of compassion? Jean is *incredibly* sad about breaking up with Tom. Just because she's the one who ended it, doesn't mean she isn't still in love with him!"

"It doesn't?" Amy asked, setting down her fries. "Why? What's their problem?"

"I don't know. It isn't any of my business," Jessica answered. "It's between Jean and Tom. But I think as Jean's friends we owe her a little kindness, Amy. How can you just announce you want to date Tom before she's even gotten used to being without him?"

Amy looked stung. "Sor-ry. I guess you can't consider the fact that I misjudged the situation a little? After all, it's easy to see how I could've gotten the wrong impression."

"You're *always* misjudging," Jessica said angrily. Suddenly she remembered how upset she had been at the Beach Disco Saturday night. And she had just waited twenty minutes for Amy for lunch. Jessica did not like being treated so carelessly, and her own pique helped her leap to Jean's defense. "If you weren't thinking so much about yourself all the time, maybe you'd see how other people are feeling!"

Amy looked pale, and the table fell quiet again. None of the girls were used to serious disagreements, and the silence soon became awkward.

"Listen, I'm going to see how Jean's doing," Cara said. She picked up her lunch tray and hurried away.

Jessica's mouth was set in a firm line. She was really irritated with Amy Sutton, and she wanted her friend to know it. Her callous behavior to Jean was the last straw! The cheerleaders owed one another a certain amount of loyalty and concern. Maybe it would not have been so bad for Amy to express interest in Tom in a few weeks. But to say something now, when Jean was so obviously suffering, was incredibly inconsiderate.

In fact, Jessica was annoyed enough to find

Lila later that afternoon to talk over Amy's behavior.

"Yeah, I guess announcing her interest in Tom wasn't the most sensitive thing she could have done," Lila admitted. "But then Amy never has been Miss Tact."

Jessica grimaced. "Amy's been acting really self-centered lately. Don't you think there's something we could do to make her calm down a little?"

"Well, we could pay a little less attention to her," Lila suggested. "Maybe all she needs is a bit of the cold-shoulder treatment."

"Maybe," Jessica said judiciously.

It certainly seemed worth a try.

Two

Monday afternoon in sociology class, Amy stared at the essay on her desk. This was a disaster. She had expected a B, a C at the worst. Not a failing grade! With dismay she read Ms. Jacobi's comments written on the bottom of the page.

"Amy—I've been concerned about your writing all semester, and this paper fully justifies my concern. The essay is poorly organized and shows very little thought. I'd like you to arrange a conference with me as soon as possible."

Amy bit her lip and tears sprung to her eyes. She had been pulling a B− in sociology, not exactly a stellar grade, but OK. But this failing grade was going to devastate her average. And a terrible average was not going to thrill her parents, that was for sure.

After class, Amy waited till most of the students had left before approaching Ms. Jacobi's

12

desk. Ms. Jacobi was generally well liked by the students. She looked up at Amy with a welcoming expression.

"You and I need to go over this paper in depth," Ms. Jacobi told her.

Amy nodded. She wasn't looking forward to that one little bit.

"But I will say a few things now. The biggest problem with this paper is that you seem to be writing on a topic you know nothing about," Ms. Jacobi continued. "You chose to write about social work. Tell me something. Have you ever done any social work?"

"Me?" Amy was astonished.

Ms. Jacobi laughed. "I thought not. Amy, I have an idea. There's a well-established clinic right here in Sweet Valley that has asked local schools to seek out student volunteers. The clinic needs people two days a week for a few hours after school to answer the hotlines, sit in on some group counseling, and work a little with troubled children. I think very highly of this clinic, and I have a feeling you might enjoy working there. I'd be willing to make a deal with you. Instead of rewriting this paper from book research, how would you like to sign up as a volunteer for the next few weeks, and then write about your experience? The clinic will train you, of course."

Amy blinked. "Uh . . ." She wasn't sure what to say. Two afternoons a week! The work might conflict with cheerleading. Not to mention shopping and going to the beach. On the other hand, she always had been a little curious about social work. She had seen a fantastic made-for-TV movie once about a social worker and had wondered how someone could be that devoted to, and serious about, helping other people. But she had never thought about it again until now.

It had not occurred to Amy that she should have written about something she had some experience in, or that if she chose to write about something new to her, she should have done some serious reading. But if Ms. Jacobi was willing to let her trade rewriting her paper from library research for a few afternoons a week at the clinic, why not take advantage of the offer? It sounded like an easy way to raise her grade. "OK," she said with a shrug and a smile.

Ms. Jacobi took off her glasses and looked closely at Amy. "It isn't an easy place to work, Amy. Some young people need a lot of support. But I think you'll learn to value the time you put in at the clinic." She pulled a pad of paper before her and began to write. "I'll tell you what. I'm going to call Kathy Henry, who heads up the clinic, and tell her that I've told you to drop by tomorrow afternoon. The clinic is called Project Youth, and it's right downtown. Here's all the information you'll need," she said, handing Amy a piece of paper.

Amy nodded. She was eager to leave the classroom and Ms. Jacobi's earnest eyes. "Thanks," she said, stuffing the slip of paper into her bag and turning away.

She could hardly believe she had gotten her-self into such a situation. Project Youth? Well, right now, anything was better than failing sociology!

Amy didn't want to think too hard about what it would be like to volunteer at the clinic. In fact, what she really wanted right now was some company. Maybe Jessica would go with her to the mall.

She found Jessica at her locker, digging furi-ously in search of her math book. "Wow, what a pigpen," Amy said. Her voice was full of false cheer as she inspected her friend's messy locker.

Jessica turned around and scowled. "Amy, do you mind? I happen to be in a hurry."

Amy felt stung. She really had not intended to say anything nasty about the state of Jessica's locker. The words had just sort of flown out. "I wanted to know . . ." She shifted her books. "I was just wondering if you felt like going shopping."

Jessica shook her head. "Sorry, but I've got a dentist's appointment, and I'm already late for it." She took hold of the locker door, slammed it shut, and raced off without a backward glance. Amy bit her lip.

OK, she told herself brightly. She would go home and wait for her mother to arrive from the TV station. Maybe they could go to the mall together before dinner.

On her way home, Amy thought uneasily about Jessica's brush-off. It had not made her feel very good, particularly coming right after her meeting with Ms. Jacobi. *I need something new and really nice in my life,* she thought. An image of Tom McKay appeared in her mind's eye. Amy had never had a boyfriend, not a real one. She had dates all the time, but never anything really steady. Even Amy's relationship with Bruce Patman, though long-term, had not been true love, nothing like the relationship Elizabeth Wakefield had with Todd Wilkins. Maybe it was time for a change.

The Suttons lived in a pretty, mission-style house on a tree-lined street in central Sweet Valley. Amy opened the front door and called hello. No one answered. That was not unusual. Her father was a freelance photographer and he was often hard at work in his darkroom at the back of the house. Maybe he had gone to his office downtown to finish developing some prints. In any case, he was not around and Amy knew her mother probably would not be home for a while yet.

Amy wandered around the house, looking for a diversion. She turned on the TV but the late-afternoon soaps bored her today. "There's nothing to *do* here," she grumbled. She sat down on the couch and stared out the window. She felt awful, really down in the dumps. This was not like her!

"Hey, when did you get home?" Mr. Sutton exclaimed as he came into the living room, wiping his hands on a towel. He smelled of the chemicals he used to develop photographs.

Amy mustered up a grin. "Ten minutes ago, I guess."

Mr. Sutton was a handsome man in his mid-forties, his dark hair just streaked at the sides with gray. "I got some great news today from my agent," he told her proudly. "The contract with the publishers has been finalized. I can go ahead with my book!" Mr. Sutton had been working for several years on a collection of his photographs.

"Daddy, that's wonderful!" Amy jumped up to give him a hug. "When will the book be published?"

"Oh, not for ages, sometime next year probably. And now that I know it'll definitely be published, there's a lot of revision work I want to do. I'm really not satisfied with the first part at all. In fact, that's what I was working on all afternoon. I'm rewriting the introduction, trying to get a sense of how it's going to look in print."

Amy tried to smile at her father's enthusiasm. He sounded just like a kid on his birthday. "I'm really happy for you, Dad," she repeated. The truth was, she felt a bit jealous, left out. She thought her voice sounded a little hollow, but if it did, Mr. Sutton didn't notice.

"Listen, your mother called, and she's going to have to work a little late tonight. Maybe you and I could order a pizza later, OK?"

"Won't she be home for dinner?" Amy demanded.

"I'm not sure. I think a game had to be rescheduled, something like that. She didn't say when she'd be home." Mr. Sutton looked as though he was dying to get back to his darkroom.

"Maybe *I* could make dinner. We could wait until Mom gets home and all eat together," Amy suggested.

"Sure, if that's what you feel like doing," Mr. Sutton replied.

Amy nodded. "Go on back to work, Daddy. Let me see what I can come up with."

One of the golden rules in the Sutton household was that the family always tried to have dinner together. Though Amy was the first to grumble when she had a date to get ready for, she really did like the tradition. Amy was a little surprised when her father so casually dismissed the issue tonight. Well, she had changed his mind. She would go ahead and make dinner for all of them.

Amy poked unhappily through her mother's cookbooks. None of the recipes looked terribly easy to follow.

It was obvious that Amy's mother had not been to the store for several days. But Amy found a package of chicken in the freezer. There was also a bottle of barbecue sauce in the refrigerator. How hard could it be to grill chicken? As she washed some lettuce for a salad, Amy felt a few loyal pangs toward her parents. Though she grumbled about her mother's not being home all the time, Amy really was proud of her mother's career. How many other kids could boast having a TV sportscaster for a mother? And her father's news about his book was pretty wonderful, too.

While she worked in the kitchen, Amy wondered if Tom McKay would like her parents. She was sure they would like him. He was exactly the kind of guy she imagined they would want her to go out with.

Her thoughts were interrupted at seven-thirty when the back door burst open and her mother came in. "Hi, sweetheart! Sorry I'm late," her mother said. She stopped short when she saw her daughter surrounded by plates and pots. "You're cooking dinner! Don't you have homework to do?"

Amy remembered Ms. Jacobi and her stomach felt funny. "No. I'm all through, Mom, and I wanted to help out."

"Well, thanks, sweetheart. That's nice of you," her mother said, flipping through the mail. "Anything new at school?"

"No, not really." Amy wished there was something exciting she could tell her mother. She certainly couldn't tell her about volunteering at Project Youth when she was only doing it to make up for flunking a paper!

"I'm exhausted," her mother continued, slipping out of her suit jacket. "We had the craziest day at the station! Let me go upstairs and change, and I'll help you with dinner," she added, looking at the platter of chicken Amy was getting ready to take out to the grill.

Amy was glad she had started dinner. It made her feel as though she was contributing something at home. Sometimes it was hard having parents who were so accomplished. Amy was often asked what it was like to be Dyan Sutton's daughter and she always came up with good answers. She boasted about the famous people her mother knew, that sort of thing. But she also felt kind of pressured. Her mother was a very glamorous woman, and she seemed to have her life in perfect control. Amy's father adored her, they had lots of friends and a great social life, in addition to her career. Amy could not imagine herself ever having it all together the way her mother did.

Mr. Sutton came into the kitchen. "Let me help you with that, Amy," he said, following her out to the grill in the backyard. He inspected the chicken on the platter. "Did you defrost the chicken?"

Amy squinted at the chicken. Come to think of it, it *had* felt a little icy when she had painted it with barbecue sauce. But she was sure the pieces would thaw fast enough once on the grill. "Of course, Daddy," she said reproachfully.

"OK, then. Looks as if you have everything set here. I'll go say hi to your mother."

Amy barely heard him. She frowned down at the chicken pieces, which looked more and more like red-coated blocks of ice. "I hope this works," she muttered as she tossed the first piece onto the flaming barbecue.

"I think we ought to make a toast," Mrs. Sutton said as she pulled a chair up to the patio table that was set for dinner. She beamed at her

20

husband. "Congratulations, sweetheart. Here's to the most talented photographer I know!"

"Here, here," Amy echoed.

"Amy," her father said as he tried to cut into a chicken breast, "are you sure you defrosted this. It seems a little . . ."

Amy reddened. "I told you I did, Daddy," she said fiercely. She knew she was being defensive, but she could not help but feel hurt. After all the work she had put into getting dinner together for them tonight, why did he have to be so critical?

Mrs. Sutton took a tiny bite of her piece, then switched rapidly to her salad. "Delicious salad, Amy," she said.

Amy sat back in her seat. She felt miserable. It was a relief when her parents went back to discussing their work. At least for a while it was.

Mrs. Sutton described how hectic and how exciting her day had been. Through her hard work and ingenuity, the network had wrangled an interview with Stan Maverick, the hottest rookie for the Pistols. She had been on the phone with a million different people, settling the details. "But it was thrilling," she added, her blue eyes sparkling. "And I got to talk to Stan for several minutes. He promised he'd try to get me an interview with the team's coach."

Amy's father hung on his wife's every word. He obviously thought she was brilliant and fascinating, and who could blame him? Why bother listening to Amy when he could listen to Dyan Sutton instead?

21

Next, Mrs. Sutton pumped her husband for information about his book contract. Mr. Sutton was usually fairly reticent about the business side of his work, but tonight he could not squelch his excitement. "It's incredible. I might actually see *royalties* from this project. The publisher wants to do a big promotional tour. I may have to go to New York next month to meet with my editor."

Mrs. Sutton's eyes lit up. "That's great! I think *I* may go to New York, too. There's a media and sports conference I should attend. Maybe we can combine the two trips!"

Great, Amy thought, pushing her inedible chicken from one side of the plate to the other. That was just great. Maybe they should just stay in New York and forget all about her. She felt about as interesting as the half-frozen chicken in front of her.

As if on cue, both her parents looked at each other, then turned to Amy.

"It was very thoughtful of you to make dinner tonight, Amy," her mother said.

"We haven't heard about *your* day," her father added.

Amy thought fast. "You know what happened that was really funny?" she asked rhetorically. "Remember those two guys I told you about, the guys who both said I was cute?" Her parents looked at her expectantly, and Amy went on. "Ralph Woodley is one of them, and the other is A. J. Morgan, Jessica's ex-boyfriend. I know I've told you about them," she added nervously.

"I don't think so." Mrs. Sutton's face was blank.

"Well, in art class, Ralph wanted to sit on the stool next to me, and so did A.J. They argued for about five minutes before the teacher told them to cut it out." Amy giggled at the memory. Neither parent commented and she added, "See, they both wanted to be near me, and if the teacher hadn't stepped in they would have kidded around the whole class long!"

"They must have annoyed your art teacher," Mr. Sutton said dryly.

Mrs. Sutton didn't say a word. Amy felt terrible. She was failing sociology, her best friends were angry with her, and her parents seemed happier ignoring her. What else could go wrong?

"Amy? Can I come in?" Mrs. Sutton knocked gently on Amy's door. It was ten-thirty, and Amy was trying to read her history assignment for the next day. But none of it was really sinking in. It was hard to concentrate after such a bad day, and she was very sleepy.

"Sure, Mom." When Amy was younger she loved the before-bed talks with her mother. She felt nostalgic now as her mother crossed the room and sat down on the bed. Mrs. Sutton smiled fondly at her daughter.

"Amy, we haven't talked seriously in a long time. I know it's really my fault. I'm always so busy at work. So I hope you don't think I'm interfering now," her mother said softly. "But I've been thinking about you a lot lately. You have some big decisions to make in the very near future. And at dinner tonight it struck me that maybe you haven't been thinking very seriously about them. College isn't all that far away. You'll start applying in the fall. Have you given any thought to what you want to be, or where you want to go?"

Amy opened her mouth as if to speak. But before she could answer, her mother continued. "I think it's time for you to get more serious about your life, Amy. Your father thinks so, too. It's great to fool around and have fun, but there's more to life than that. Don't you think it's time to focus yourself a little? To ask yourself some important questions?"

Amy felt a lump forming in her throat.

"I just want you to be happy," her mother continued. She took one of Amy's hands and stroked it. "I'd like to see you a little more . . . decisive, I suppose. I don't mean to sound harsh. You know I want your happiness more than anything else."

Amy choked back tears. "Thanks, Mom. I'll . . . uh, I'll think about it." Mrs. Sutton kissed Amy's cheek and left the room.

Great. On top of failing sociology, and not doing too well in any of her other classes, her mother was going to start pressuring her. That is, when she wasn't ignoring her.

Obviously, her parents were suddenly so concerned because of the story she had told them at dinner. They knew Amy rarely went out with the same guy twice. If she had a boyfriend, they would be sure to take her more seriously. They would see her as more grown-up.

That was it, an easy place to start. She would find herself a serious boyfriend, one her parents would be impressed with. Someone popular and talented, just like them. Someone like —Tom McKay.

Amy was resolved. She would make Tom hers and the rest of her growing up would follow.

Three

On Tuesday, Elizabeth could hardly wait to see Enid at lunchtime. "Hi, stranger!" she said cheerfully as she slid into the seat next to her friend. Winston Egbert, unofficial clown of the junior class, was sitting with Enid, as were Maria Santelli, Winston's girlfriend, and Todd Wilkins. Elizabeth had hardly seen Enid in the past two days.

"Where have you been? I bet you've been busy planning what you're going to do with that fabulous cousin of yours when he gets here," Elizabeth teased.

Jake Farrell, Enid's cousin from San Francisco, was coming to visit Sweet Valley. Enid had just gotten the news last week, and she was very excited. Jake was a legend in her family, and if he lived up to all reports, Elizabeth knew his visit was going to be exciting.

"Mom and I have been doing some heavy-duty cleaning. You know how mothers get when houseguests are coming." Enid rolled her eyes. "So I've had to spend every spare minute catching up on homework. I spent yesterday's lunch period in the library! Honestly, if Mom finds one more thing to clean, I'm going to call Jake and beg him to come right now instead of this weekend!"

Elizabeth's eyes brightened. "So he's coming this weekend?" As of the last report, Jake had not known when he could get away. He was a serious tennis player, with a chance to join the pro circuit next year, and his coach was strict about letting him take time off from his practice schedule.

"Yeah. Jake finally talked his coach into letting him come visit. And it's a long weekend for us, remember? We have Monday off because of the teachers' conference." Enid's green eyes shone. "I can hardly believe he's really going to be here. You guys are going to just adore him," she promised. "He's smart, he's funny, he's cool. He's got a real presence. Everybody likes him."

Elizabeth laughed. "Well, Jessica is a fan of his already. That picture of Jake you showed her last week really bowled her over."

"Well, he *is* cute," Enid said loyally. "At least he was the last time I saw him, when he was fifteen. And I'm sure two years have only made him cuter."

"I can hardly wait to meet this paragon, this demigod," Winston said drolly. "Maybe we should have a parade in his honor."

"Oh, you," Maria said playfully. "You just don't like having to share the attention around here."

"Yeah. I've noticed Elizabeth's sister isn't drooling over *my* picture," Winston said in a voice of mock-sorrow.

Everyone laughed and Maria pretended to pummel him.

"Seriously, we ought to think about planning some fun things to do this weekend," Enid said.

"Later." Elizabeth narrowed her eyes across the lunchroom. "Don't look now but Jessica and Lila are headed this way. And if I know my sister, she's not going to be able to restrain herself from asking you about Jake!"

Jessica and Lila strolled by a moment later. They each wore an air of assumed nonchalance that made Enid and Elizabeth giggle.

"Hi, Liz," Jessica called out coyly.

"Hi, Jess," Elizabeth answered, hiding her amusement. Jessica had always considered Enid Rollins too sedate for words, and waiting for her twin to invent an excuse for joining their table now was pretty funny.

"Hey, Enid," Lila said, stopping abruptly as if the thought had just occurred to her. "That cousin of yours—what's his name again—Drake, Blake. . . ."

"Jake."

"Oh, yeah! Jake!" Lila and Jessica each grabbed a chair and pulled it over to the table. "Jake. I love that name," Lila drawled. "So, when do we get to meet him?"

28

"This weekend, as a matter of fact."

Lila and Jessica stared at each other and each let out a little shriek. "Omigod. This *weekend*," Jessica cried.

"I've got to go to the mall. I don't have a thing to wear," Lila moaned.

Enid burst out laughing. "You two are incredible. You haven't even met him yet. How do you know you'll even like him?"

"Oh, I can tell right away," Lila protested. "I knew the minute I saw his picture."

"Me, too," Jessica seconded. "I don't know, something about that gorgeous build, that incredible face."

"I can't stand this anymore," Winston declared. "Let me see this photograph before I go put a bag over my head."

Enid grinned. "I've got it here somewhere." She reached for her purse and poked around inside it.

"I saw you put it back in your wallet last week," Lila said helpfully.

"You're right. Here it is." Enid took out a small snapshot. "This picture is two years old, though. I'm sure he's changed."

Winston craned his neck for a look, but it was hard to see much of Jake with Lila and Jessica sticking their heads in his way.

"He's *so* gorgeous." Jessica breathed deeply. "How does he stay so tan, living in San Francisco?"

"Look at those dimples. I've never met a guy with dimples who wasn't a doll," Lila pronounced.

"And curly hair, too. He's just my type," Jessica cried.

29

Enid laughed. "Whoa! Back off, you two! For all I know, he may have a girlfriend."

The possibility seemed to stun Jessica. "He can't, or he wouldn't ever go away for a long weekend," she said vehemently.

"Right," Lila agreed. "But that doesn't mean he won't have a girlfriend after this weekend. Enid, this cousin of yours is way too cute to keep under wraps. You have to be sure he gets lots of public exposure!"

"I can see it now," Jessica crooned. "I'll be up in San Francisco every other weekend."

"I love a guy who's serious about tennis," Lila added. "It's so, you know. So *rich*."

"Maybe you can buy him some clay courts as a welcome gift, Lila," Winston wisecracked.

"Hey," a familiar voice interrupted, "is there any room here, or do I have to eat this gruesome-looking lunch standing up?"

Elizabeth looked up to see Amy Sutton standing uncertainly near the table, holding her tray. "There's plenty of room. Todd, squeeze over," she said.

Elizabeth noticed that neither Jessica nor Lila said a word.

"What are you all looking at?" Amy asked, unloading the food from her tray.

"Enid's cousin is coming to visit this weekend. We're looking at his picture," Elizabeth explained, noticing again that neither Jessica nor Lila volunteered an explanation. Were they deliberately giving Amy the cold shoulder?

"Oh, yeah. I saw it before. He's cute," Amy said.

30

"Hands off, Amy." Lila smirked. "Hey, remember what happened when *my* cousin came to town?" she asked everyone at the table.

Enid blushed, and everyone fell silent.

Elizabeth could see that Amy looked uncomfortable, and she felt sorry for her. It was an awkward memory. Soon after Amy had moved back to Sweet Valley, Lila's cousin Christopher had come to visit and had created a real stir. Lila had given a big party in his honor, and Amy had chased him the whole night, even though it was clear to everyone but Amy that Christopher was not in the least bit interested in her.

In fact, Christopher had discovered he had an old friend at the party. He and Enid had gone to summer camp together several years before, and he had much preferred chatting with Enid about old times to dancing with Amy. There had been an embarrassing scene for Amy in the end. Elizabeth was a little surprised Lila had recalled the incident so publicly.

"Just keep Jake away from Amy, that's all I can say," Lila continued.

Amy's face was red. "I'm not going to make a play for Jake, Lila," she said hotly. "I happen to be a very different person now than I was then."

Jessica and Lila burst into giggles, and Amy looked hurt.

"Listen, I need help in planning some fun things to do while Jake's here," Enid said quickly, breaking the tension at the table. "I'm going to get some ice cream. Then we can get down to some serious scheming."

31

*   *   *

Amy poked unhappily at her salad. She would have felt a lot better if she had sat all by herself.

Some friends, she thought glumly, watching Jessica and Lila put their heads together and giggle as they shared some remark about Jake Farrell's photograph.

As if Amy were really planning to go after Jake! What her friends did not understand was that the *new* Amy Sutton wanted a serious relationship, not just a weekend fling. And she had already started working on it. She had seen Tom McKay that morning in study hall and had given him her most dazzling smile. Sure enough, he had smiled back at her.

Amy was doing things differently this time. She was not going to rush. She was going to take things slowly and with determination. Just wait until her friends and parents saw she had a steady boyfriend. They would be sure to stop treating her like such a flake!

Enid came back to the table, her hands clutching several ice-cream bars which she distributed among the others. "OK, guys, let's get serious. Jake gets in on Friday afternoon and leaves Monday. Help me think of some ways to show him a good time in Sweet Valley."

Amy decided to show Jessica and Lila she was not going to hold a grudge against them for having teased her in public. "How about having a party, like Lila did? That's a great way to introduce him to a lot of people."

Jessica made a face. "We already said we don't want a rerun of Lila's party, Amy. How

32

do we know you're not going to steal Jake, like you tried to steal Christopher!"

Amy was stung. Hadn't they teased her about that night enough? Couldn't they let up? Obviously, rising above their tactics was not going to work. Jessica and Lila were out to get her.

"Cut it out, you guys," she muttered.

Jessica didn't notice Amy's genuine embarrassment. "Come on, Amy, don't lose your sense of humor. We know you too well." She began to tick off on her fingers the number of guys Amy had already dated that year. "Let's see . . . Peter DeHaven, Bruce Patman, Ken Matthews, Scott Trost. . . ."

Amy was quickly losing her appetite. "I thought we were supposed to be helping Enid, not destroying my credibility," she said, trying to keep her voice steady.

"Yeah, lighten up, Jess," Maria reproached.

Jessica sniffed. "I don't see why Amy can't take a little teasing."

Everybody fell silent. Amy stared down at her plate.

Enid cleared her throat and picked up her pencil. "It might be fun to have a party on Sunday night. After all, we don't have school on Monday."

"How about getting together at the Beach Disco on Saturday night. Does Jake like to dance?" Winston asked.

"As far as I know. Remember, I haven't seen him in two years," Enid replied. "But knowing Jake, he'd love that. Let's plan that, then. A get-together at the Beach Disco on Saturday, and a party at my house on Sunday night."

"Perfect. I can hardly wait," Lila pronounced.

The next ten minutes were filled with talk of the weekend. Once or twice Amy tried to make a comment, but no one really seemed to notice. *What's going on here?* she wondered. Usually, Amy was the center of attention, sharing the stage with Jessica and Lila. Now, nobody even noticed she was alive.

It would be different if I had a boyfriend, she thought fiercely, sneaking an envious glance at Elizabeth and Todd. *It's obvious I can't rely on my friends.* Elizabeth and Todd were so happy together. Todd seemed to anticipate everything Elizabeth needed. He even got up to get her something to drink! And she could tell they were holding hands under the table.

That was what Amy wanted. Someone to cuddle up with at football games, someone to take long walks with on the beach. No more flirting and chasing and pursuing and getting herself in weird situations. She wanted something steady, something *serious*. Someone who would love her for who she was.

"Listen, guys, will you excuse me? I've got some studying to do," Amy said as she got up from the table.

Jessica waved indifferently and Lila nodded. "Bye, Amy," Enid and Elizabeth said in unison.

Amy turned away quickly. *Just wait*, she vowed. *They won't treat me this way once I've gotten things off the ground with Tom!*

Amy never went to the library during lunch period. But that morning in study hall she had overheard Tom tell a friend that he was way behind in his homework because of tennis practice, and that he was going to have to start using lunch periods to catch up.

Amy spotted Tom across the room and her stomach did a tiny dive. Tom was incredibly cute. He was tall, tanned, with short blond hair and a casual but stylish way of dressing that Amy admired. She liked everything about Tom. He had every single one of the qualities on her "list." He was athletic, he was popular, he was good-looking. Perfect boyfriend material.

Tom was sitting alone at a corner table, books spread out before him. Amy approached him somewhat tentatively. She waited for him to look up and notice her.

She cleared her throat loudly and still he didn't look up. Frowning, Amy pulled out a chair and thumped her books down on his table.

Tom looked up briefly, and then back down at his notebook.

"Hi, Tom," Amy whispered. "What are you doing here?"

He looked up reluctantly. "Uh, I've got some homework to catch up on," he whispered in answer to her question.

"Me, too. Isn't it the worst?" Amy said sympathetically.

Tom nodded. He didn't seem eager to carry on a conversation.

"Do you always work in the library?" Amy persisted.

Tom ran his hand through his hair. "No. But I really need to get this assignment finished, Amy. I'll talk to you later, OK?"

Amy nodded. "I'll talk to you later," Tom had said. That wasn't such a bad start. Although she was used to getting what she wanted right away, Amy knew she had to be patient with Tom. He was a bit shy, and he might still be feeling vulnerable if Jean had hurt his feelings.

Amy sneaked appreciative little glances at Tom as she pretended to read her Spanish book. He was gorgeous, no denying it. She could hardly wait until they were boyfriend and girlfriend. Maybe they would have study dates! *That* ought to make her parents happy! Amy began to daydream about what it would be like once they were really serious about each other. They would spend every weekend together, she'd have a date for every special occasion, and no more feeling lonely or left out. A boyfriend took care of those awful feelings!

About ten minutes later Tom closed his book in exasperation. "I've got to get going," he whispered as he gathered his books together.

Amy was out of her seat in a second. "Me, too," she said, flashing him a bright smile. And before Tom had gotten half a yard away from the table, Amy had fallen into step beside him.

Four

After school Amy headed for her first appointment at Project Youth. She felt a little apprehensive as she neared the modest brick building that housed the clinic. She was sure the last thing she would be any good at was social work. She knew herself well enough to realize that she was not particularly interested in other people's problems. And lately she had had enough crises of her own to worry about. How could she possibly help other people with theirs?

Still, there was something about social work that intrigued Amy. As she approached the clinic, she remembered the movie she had seen, the one that had so impressed her. The heroine had managed to make people's lives better. To Amy's surprise she had been very moved by the story.

But *this* was not a movie, she reminded herself. This was real life, and this clinic looked *all* too real, at least from the outside.

Amy opened the front door cautiously. The scene that greeted her was friendly and relaxed, not at all like what Amy had supposed a clinic would look like. In a room to her right, a group of teenagers, all about thirteen or fourteen, were playing cards, listening to music, and talking. A small woman of about thirty got up from her place with the group and gave Amy a big smile. "You must be Amy Sutton. Your teacher told me you'd be coming. I'm Kathy Henry. Let me tell you a little about what we do."

Kathy gave Amy a tour of the clinic. As they went she explained who they were and how they worked. "Most of the people who come here are teenagers. Some are as young as ten or eleven, some as old as eighteen, but most are in junior high. They come for all sorts of reasons. Some are having trouble in school or at home. Some have problems with drinking or drugs. Some are depressed. We hear all kinds of stories here and our most important rule is that we respect each other no matter what."

Amy nodded. She liked this woman. She seemed very real and down-to-earth, not at all condescending.

"We have another volunteer from your school. He started with us last year. He's been working on the hot lines, answering phone calls from teens in trouble. If you'd like, you could work with him for a while, that is, while you're undergoing the introductory training sessions. Each session is an hour and you'll need four hours of training before you can solo on the phones. In fact, a session is starting in a few minutes. Why not jump on board now?"

"Sure." Amy was scared. She could not imagine answering a phone call from someone in trouble. What advice could *she* possibly have to give? Maybe she'd be given a manual in addition to her training, a book that held all the answers.

An hour later, Kathy escorted Amy to the switchboard.

"Barry?" Kathy called to a slender, dark-haired boy who looked familiar to Amy. "Barry, this is Amy. She's just had her first hour of training and she's going to be working with you for a while. Help her out, OK?" Kathy waved and headed off.

"I know you," Barry said, his eyes lighting up. "You're Amy Sutton, right?"

Amy nodded. She didn't really know Barry, and frankly, he didn't look all that thrilling. Dark curly hair, glasses. Maybe he would be cute if he sat up a little straighter and got contact lenses.

"I'm on the tennis team," he explained.

"Oh. With Tom McKay?" Amy demanded.

"Yeah." Barry looked away. "Well, I guess we should get to work. Let me show you how to work the switchboard."

As Amy took a seat next to him, she congratulated herself on her good luck. If she got friendly with Barry, maybe he would put in a good word for her with Tom!

"What made you sign up to help here?" Barry asked.

"Oh—" Amy was about to make a flippant

remark, but something held her back. "I'm interested in social work. I wanted to learn more about this clinic." She was afraid she sounded uncertain and vague.

Barry shook his head admiringly. "That's pretty impressive. You sound like the sort of person who already knows what you want to do with your life." When Amy shook her head, Barry continued. "Most people only volunteer for some selfish reason. Like me. I'm in this because my little brother, Jerry, has a lot of problems, and I'm hoping my work at the clinic will give me some pointers on how to cope with him."

Amy fiddled with her hair. "Yeah, well, that doesn't sound so selfish to me." She glanced at the complicated-looking phone system in front of her. The first training session had covered how to use the phones and what to say to the callers, but Amy still wasn't feeling very confident. "So, now what?"

"When someone calls, you tell them you're a telephone counselor with Project Youth, that their call is confidential and they can say whatever they want because Project Youth isn't about judgments, it's about understanding." Barry seemed so self-assured, he made her feel less awkward.

Amy nodded. "That sounds pretty easy."

"And then . . ." Barry shrugged. "You listen. Every call is different. That's the hardest thing to remember, that each call comes from someone who's in real pain. The person wouldn't be calling if he or she didn't really need someone to listen."

Amy swallowed. It all sounded awfully serious. What if she blew it? "Isn't there, I don't know, some kind of book I can read that will tell me what to say to people?"

Barry laughed. "That's one of the great things about this clinic. Books don't do any good here. Project Youth is about life, not about research. You'll learn that through your training." Barry could tell that Amy was still concerned.

"I'll help you with the first few calls. I'll get on the line, too, and afterward, I'll go over the calls with you and tell you what I think. But listen, no one's got a formula. You've got to find your own way." Barry smiled encouragingly.

Amy took a deep breath. A red light flashed on the phone. "Pick it up," Barry urged.

Amy did. "Hello, this is Project Youth," she said. She was surprised by how steady her voice sounded.

"Hi . . . uh . . . my name is Ellen. I'm fourteen. I think—uh . . . I think I'm in trouble. I feel really sad all the time. I don't have any friends."

Boy, Amy thought, *I can relate to this one.*

"I get really nervous in class. There's this guy. I like him a lot but he never notices me. I feel so ugly." The girl sounded close to tears.

Amy took a deep breath. "What you're feeling is normal, Ellen." Amy tried to get up her nerve to go on. "It's really hard sometimes believing in yourself when you think other people

41

don't. But believe me, you're not alone. Is there anyone close to you you can talk to?"

Barry gave her the thumbs-up sign.

"Well, I can talk to my mom. But I still get so depressed."

Amy settled back. She listened intently and was as supportive and sympathetic as she could be. It was strange at first, talking to someone who didn't know who *she* was, who didn't want to hear anything about Amy at all! But to her amazement, she enjoyed the call. When she finally hung up, after having told Ellen about the clinic and urging her to come by sometime soon, Amy felt almost triumphant.

"That was great." Barry smiled warmly.

Amy shook her head. "It's easy. Talking on the phone is one of my talents," she said.

"Don't sell yourself short. You were great with her," Barry said firmly.

Amy was embarrassed. She didn't know quite what to say. *Tell* Tom *how great I am, tell my parents how great I am,* was what she was thinking. But the phone rang again, and Amy reached for it before Barry could. She was ready to talk to another kid in trouble.

"See you Thursday," Barry said cheerfully at five o'clock when Amy gathered her things to leave. Amy nodded. She tried to ignore the way Barry was looking at her. If only you were Tom McKay, she thought.

But he wasn't. And whoever he was, Barry just wasn't her type.

*   *   *

After school on Wednesday Amy changed for cheerleading practice. She was determined to keep her spirits up. So far, it had not been a great day. Both her parents had left for work early and she had eaten breakfast alone, and at lunchtime Jessica, Lila, and Cara had disappeared on an errand, leaving her stranded again. At least cheerleading practice would be fun, she promised herself.

The other cheerleaders were already out on the field by the time Amy joined them. They were standing in a semicircle around Jean, who looked as if she had been crying.

"Sorry I'm late," Amy said.

"OK, let's get started," Robin Wilson said brusquely.

Robin, who was co-captain of the cheerleading squad with Jessica, was leading practice although she herself wouldn't be working out for a while. She was still recovering from a case of pneumonia brought on from severe weight loss, and her doctors did not think she was strong enough yet for strenuous activity. But Robin was getting stronger every day. With support and therapy, Robin had learned her weight loss was due to anorexia nervosa, an eating disorder, a phenomenon she now knew was neither uncommon nor shameful. The other cheerleaders were glad to have her back.

"You should tell Jean you're sorry. She's really bummed out about what you said about Tom the other day at lunch," Jessica said under her breath to Amy.

Amy bit her lip. Luckily, Robin was instructing them to get into formation, because she really didn't know what to say in her own defense. Jean and Tom were finished! And since when was Jessica so self-righteous about this sort of thing? The two girls had always considered "all's fair in love and war" their chief motto.

It was probably just sour grapes, Amy decided. Maybe Jessica was angry because Amy had gotten her hands on Tom before she did. Well, she couldn't waste her time worrying. If Jessica wanted to act crazy, then let her.

But Amy didn't have anywhere near as much fun at practice as she usually did. She had trouble concentrating. Her mind was a whirl of confusing thoughts. When the cheerleaders had finished the last cheer, they headed back to the locker room, eager to change and go out for ice cream. But Amy stayed behind. She wanted to watch the boys' tennis team practice. And if her friends were determined to give her the cold shoulder, why give them further opportunity?

Tom was playing singles with Barry when Amy stopped by the courts ten minutes later. When Barry dropped a ball at the sight of her, Amy was glad that she had spent so much time with him the day before.

"Amy!" He waved his racket.

She gave him a little wave she had seen once in an old movie. It seemed to charm Barry completely, and Amy grinned. Good. She was halfway there. Now, if only Tom would notice her!

Tom gave a halfhearted wave and nodded his head to Barry. "Your serve," he reminded him.

Amy spread her sweater on the grass and sat down daintily. She watched with interest as they played. Both boys were good, but Tom was a better, more powerful player. Amy noted with pleasure that he was very muscular. She liked the way he looked when he ran. Amy again began to daydream about what it would be like once they were seeing each other. She would come watch Tom play all the time. After each game they would go for a drive, maybe up to Miller's Point.

Barry's voice brought Amy out of her reverie. "I didn't know telephone counselors moonlighted as cheerleaders," he said as he walked toward her, tossing a neon-green tennis ball awkwardly in one hand. Tom walked along with Barry, wiping his face with a towel.

"Let's not talk about counseling here," Amy answered with a quick glance at Tom. She did not want her reputation ruined.

Barry looked surprised. "OK, if that's—"

Amy cut him off again. "Tom, what a great game!" she cooed as she got to her feet. "You know, I need a lot of help on my backhand. I bet you're probably far too busy to help a poor struggling cheerleader learn how to hit, right?" She spoke in her most flirtatious voice.

Tom flung his towel over his shoulder. "Well, actually, I'm pretty booked these days. I've got practice every afternoon this week. And I promised Enid I'd save some time to hit a few balls with her cousin this weekend."

Amy bit her lip. "Not even a teeny little bit of time left over?"

Barry cleared his throat. "I'll help you, Amy."

Tom looked obviously grateful, and Amy began to feel annoyed.

"I'll just wait for you," she turned to Tom, completely ignoring Barry's offer.

"If you change your mind, Amy, I'll be around," Barry called after her as she turned and walked away.

Amy shook her head. She should have known. This was just not her day. How was she ever going to get to Tom if Barry was always in the way?

Five

On Thursday afternoon Amy realized she was actually looking forward to going to Project Youth after school. Of course, if anyone had found out about her work, she would have down-played the whole thing, saying she was only doing it to make up her grade. But she *was* excited when she opened the clinic's heavy front door. Coming to the clinic was an adventure, so different from anything she had ever done before.

When she finished her training session, Barry was already on the phones. They worked to-gether side by side for about an hour before there was a lull long enough to allow them a break.

"Phew," Amy said, taking off her headset. "I had some tough ones this afternoon." She looked curiously at Barry. "How do you get used to this? It's weird talking about such heavy stuff, and then switching so quickly back to normal life."

Barry shrugged good-naturedly. "It gets easier over time. You find out that other people's problems aren't so different from your own."

Amy nodded. She had been thinking about one of the young girls who had called in that afternoon. Her name was Mindy and she was fourteen. Mindy had had a big fight with her parents and ever since then her confidence had been at an all-time low. Well, Amy could sure identify with *that*. She'd found that she was really able to comfort the girl. Maybe she actually did have a knack for this sort of work!

"Hey, you want to get a soda downstairs? Kathy always tells me it's important to take a five-minute breather," Barry said.

"Sure." Amy stretched. She was a little stiff from having sat for so long.

Barry forwarded the calls to Kathy's office. Then he and Amy walked down to the lounge. Barry fired questions at her all the way. Why was she interested in social work? Had she ever thought about being a social worker? Did she have any brothers or sisters?

Amy laughed. "This sounds like an FBI interrogation," she teased him.

Barry shook his head. "I can't help it. When I want to get to know people, I'm not always very subtle. You'll learn that about me, Amy. I'm a pretty straightforward person. I tend to say what's on my mind."

Amy took the soda he offered her. "Not me. I tend to be the opposite," she admitted. "Sometimes I hear myself saying things I just can't believe are coming out of my mouth!" She shook her head. "Sometimes I hear myself sounding flaky and I hate it. But . . ." She shrugged. "I guess it's my style."

Barry nodded. "Nothing wrong with that. You've got to know who you are and be proud of it."

Amy sat down next to Barry. It felt funny talking so honestly, particularly to a guy. It must be the welcoming atmosphere of the clinic, she told herself. She had never confided in anyone like this before, and certainly not a guy.

Come to think of it, Amy had never had a male friend before. The realization surprised her, but it was true. No brothers, no male cousins. She caught herself grinning, and realized that it was *nice* having this kind of talk with Barry. He was certainly making this internship more enjoyable. And, of course, he might also help her get closer to Tom. They certainly seemed to be good friends.

"Still looking for some help with your tennis game?" Barry asked suddenly.

"Well . . ." Amy dropped her eyes. "Actually, I was just kind of using that as an excuse. I want to get to know Tom McKay better," she blurted out. There. She had said it.

Barry looked a bit pained. After a minute he cleared his throat. "Well, that's honest of you."

"You two are good friends, right?" Amy continued.

Barry nodded. "Yeah. He's a great guy," he said quietly.

"He really is, isn't he?" Amy mused. "Listen, do you think you could help me out a little. Kind of hint to him that I'm interested?"

Barry stared hard at a poster on the opposite wall. "Sure," he said at last. "I don't know how good I am at matchmaking, but I can pass along the message."

Amy felt like hugging him. "Thanks a million," she said, grabbing his hand and squeezing it. She barely even noticed that Barry turned beet red and quickly looked away.

Elizabeth and Todd arrived at the Dairi Burger at about seven-thirty on Friday evening. "I can't wait to meet Jake," Elizabeth said as they parked Todd's BMW in front of the cheerful old dive of a hamburger place.

"Me, too. He sounds terrific," Todd answered.

Enid had rounded up several friends to help her welcome her cousin to town, but news of Jake's arrival had spread so quickly that the whole place seemed packed with curious classmates. Elizabeth spotted Enid right away. She was seated at a corner booth with Winston, Maria, and Tom McKay. Next to Tom sat a taller, more handsome version of the Jake Elizabeth had seen in Enid's photograph.

Elizabeth and Todd hurried over to join their friends.

"Oh, Jake, I want you to meet two of my favorite people in the whole world!" Enid's green eyes were shining as she made the introductions.

"Well, if you're two of my cousin's favorite

people, I feel honored to meet you!" Jake smiled and offered his hand.

Elizabeth and Todd slipped into the booth and Todd asked Jake about living in San Francisco.

"It's a really great town. There's a lot happening in the arts, as well as in the local communities. And the city is just so beautiful," Jake said enthusiastically. He mentioned some of the things he liked best about the Bay Area—the bridges, the lovely hills, the wonderful restaurants.

Elizabeth smiled as she listened to Jake. He was every bit as captivating as Enid had promised. He was tall and slender, with dark curly hair and wonderful hazel eyes that twinkled intelligently. Elizabeth liked what he was wearing, too—a sports jacket over a white shirt, opened casually at the neck, and linen trousers. Jake managed to look trendy and casual at the same time.

"I hear the tennis scene in San Francisco is pretty different than it is down here in southern California," Tom observed.

Jake's eyes brightened. "Right. You're the tennis player Enid's determined to have ruin my reputation tomorrow."

Everyone laughed. "That's me. But from what I hear about your game, I'll be lucky to come away with my racket intact." Tom grinned.

"Listen, do you know a guy named Eddie Herbert? He does some coaching at UCLA, and he's pretty big on the tennis scene around L.A.," Jake asked.

Tom nodded. "Of course I know Eddie! He's a local legend."

"He's a great friend of mine," Jake said modestly.

"Hey," Jessica called brightly as she approached the booth, her face set with a determined smile. "Any room for Lila and me, or do we have to take a number to meet the famous Jake Farrell?"

It took a fair amount of shifting around to squeeze both Jessica and Lila in the booth, but Jessica managed to chatter the entire time, her eyes fixed steadfastly on Enid's cousin.

"I think it was very unfair of you to sit in such a tiny booth! The rest of the Sweet Valley crowd will never get to talk to you." Jessica smiled coyly.

"Enid," Lila said sternly, "how could you feed your cousin Dairi Burger hamburgers on his very first night in Sweet Valley! I think you need a real meal, Jake. My father—I'm sure you've heard of him, George Fowler—was just telling me about this wonderful little French restaurant not far from here. I could take you there later, if you'd like."

Jake put up his hand. "Whoa! You sure know how to make a guy feel welcome," he joked. "Thanks for the invitation, Lila, but this place is exactly what I hoped for tonight."

Lila looked a little hurt but Jessica rushed in with another plan.

"I know. We could take you for a tour of Sweet Valley. There's a lot to see here," she said eagerly. "Of course, my little Fiat Spider only fits two. . . ."

Elizabeth nudged her sister in the ribs. *"Your little Fiat Spider?"* she repeated incredulously. She and Jessica shared the car, or at least they were supposed to share it. Sharing was not Jessica's strong point.

"Listen, we'll have plenty of time to get to know each other this weekend," Jake said good-naturedly. "Anyway, I want to do some catching up with Enid later tonight. And I need to get a good night's sleep. I don't want to make a fool of myself on the courts tomorrow!" Jake smiled at Tom, and everyone at the table settled down to hamburgers and conversation.

It was Enid's idea to play doubles the next morning. Elizabeth did not really feel up to playing with either Tom or Jake. She knew they were both considered excellent players. But Enid insisted they play just for fun.

Enid, Elizabeth, Jake, and Tom managed a few games together as a foursome, and they all did have fun. Elizabeth was paired with Jake, who was the most gracious partner imaginable. He praised her when she successfully returned a shot, and reassured her when she missed.

But after three games, it was obvious the boys wanted to play each other.

"That's OK. We'll be the cheering section," Enid said as she sat down on the grass.

Elizabeth sat down beside her. "Jake's really great," she said. "I didn't think anyone could live up to your description, but Jake really does. He seems like the kind of guy everyone likes."

Enid nodded. "Yeah. He's always been like that, really popular without trying. He's the kind of guy who goes out and buys a really weird watch, just because he likes it. And then all of a sudden, everyone he knows wants one! He's very sure of himself."

Elizabeth nodded and turned her attention to the court. The boys were well matched. Jake was the better player, but Tom made him work for every point. Tom's speed and force were as impressive as Jake's astonishing placement. It took hard work for Jake to take the first set, 7 to 5.

"Whew. This guy is *good*," Jake called to Enid and Elizabeth.

Tom grinned. "Get back on the court, Farrell! This time I'm not going to let you off so easy!"

"It's nice to see Tom looking a little more like himself," Elizabeth whispered to Enid. "He's seemed so upset since he and Jeanie broke up."

"I know," Enid agreed. "I'm glad he and Jake get along so well."

Before too long the girls were discussing plans for the party at the Beach Disco that evening. When Jake had narrowly taken the second set, the four decided to go to Guido's for pizza.

"I feel a little left out," Elizabeth said to Enid. Jake and Tom were deep in a discussion about tennis rackets.

"I know. Guys and sports!" Enid shrugged cheerfully and studied Guido's menu.

Tom and Jake seemed to have an amazing

amount in common. During lunch they discovered that they were both fans of science fiction. Tom had just finished reading a book by an author Jake had admired since he was twelve. They were also both jazz freaks. "I can't believe it. It's too weird," Tom said, shaking his head. "Jake, you can't tell me you've got the 1959 version of that trumpet solo. You know, I'd been looking for it for years and I just found a recording two weeks ago at a garage sale!"

At times the discussion opened up to include Elizabeth and Enid, but it quickly returned to the boys' favorite topic: tennis.

"You know, Jake, I feel as if I've met you somewhere before," Tom mused. "You're sure you weren't at the L.A. tennis course two summers ago?"

Jake shook his head. "Wrong guy. You must be mixing me up with someone else."

Elizabeth knew what Tom meant. Jake *did* seem familiar somehow. But that was just the kind of person he was. He had an openness that made him seem like an old friend. And that was probably what made him seem familiar to Tom.

Six

Amy felt extremely out of sorts Saturday morning. Her father was hard at work on his book. Her mother had to dash off to the station for what she hoped would be just "a couple of hours" to reedit a program due to be shown the next day. Amy's guess was that she would not see her mother again until the evening at least.

Where were Jessica and Lila? Amy had called each of her friends four times. Jessica's line was busy until noon, when the Wakefields' new answering machine picked up. And there was no answer at Lila's house at all.

Amy felt confused and more than a little left out. Ever since the Suttons had moved back to Sweet Valley, Amy had always felt as if she was in the center of the action. Now, for the first time, she felt abandoned.

If only Tom and I were together, she mused as she wandered listlessly around her bedroom.

She picked up her hairbrush and stood in front of the mirror, fantasizing about being with Tom. If they were a couple, she would never again feel this lonesome. Saturday afternoons would be the perfect time for doing something really fun. And Tom would never tire of telling her how great she looked and what a special person she was.

Amy shook her head. That was still a dream world. In the real world, she was alone.

"Daddy? Do you want some lunch?" Amy called to her father at twelve-thirty.

"No thanks, sweetie. I'll grab something later when I can take a break," Mr. Sutton called back.

Amy sat alone at the kitchen table and glared at her tuna fish sandwich. What had she done to deserve being deserted?

The phone rang, and Amy lunged for it. It was Kathy Henry, from Project Youth. "Listen, Amy, we're short on staff for the phone lines this afternoon. Any chance you can come in for a few hours?"

"Sure, Kathy," she replied automatically. It felt good to know somebody needed her. Some-bod*ies*, she reminded herself as she thought of the dozens of teenagers she had spoken to on the phone lines since she had begun her volunteer work at the clinic.

"You're a godsend, Amy," Kathy said when Amy showed up at Project Youth half an hour later. "Thanks for coming down. You know, I've been listening in on your calls. You've got a real talent, Amy. I think you have what it takes to become a first-rate youth counselor one day. Of course, you'd need to take a further professional training course, but I think you're a natural."

Amy blushed. "Thanks," she murmured, suddenly shy. Usually Amy adored praise, lapped it up. But this was a different sort of praise, a kind she was not accustomed to receiving. Kathy was not praising her looks or her flirtation skills. She was giving Amy a new message, one that was not so simple to process.

"I know you're only supposed to work here for a few more weeks," Kathy continued. "But if you have any interest in staying on, I'd be happy to have you. We can't afford to pay very much, but we could certainly figure out a way to give you something. I think you'd enjoy it. If you're interested, that is."

"Thanks," Amy said again. "I'd like that. I really like working here."

When Kathy had gone off to lead a counseling session, Amy sat down at the telephone table. For a moment, all her bad feelings of the morning came flooding back. But then the first call came in. That was one of the things Amy liked best about working at the clinic. She couldn't think about her own problems for very long.

"Jessica," Elizabeth exclaimed as she stood in her sister's doorway. "You're not wearing *that* to the Beach Disco, are you?"

"Why not?" Jessica said calmly. She swiveled in front of her full-length mirror and admired her reflection. Her bright red miniskirt swirled when she turned. It was perfect for the new dance steps she had been trying out earlier with Lila. The black top *was* a little skimpier than the tops Jessica usually wore, but she liked the racy effect it created. And with the black bangles she had layered on her wrist, she knew she looked hot.

Elizabeth shook her head. "Those heels look too tall for walking, let alone dancing," she objected.

"Haven't you noticed," Jessica said as she outlined her lips with fire-engine red lipstick, "that Enid's cousin is very tall?"

"Oh, no," Elizabeth groaned. "You're not seriously going after Jake, are you?"

Jessica fluffed up her hair. "Not 'seriously,' Liz, of course not. I have nothing in mind but pure fun." She reached for a can of hair spray. "Don't look so shocked," she admonished. "If you weren't so 'serious' about Todd Wilkins, you might have noticed that Jake is a hunk! He's got so much *style*," she added. "Not like the guys around here. And he's got a great sense of humor. Don't you remember, Liz, how much fun it is just to *flirt*?"

"Of course I do." Elizabeth frowned. "But isn't Jake going to get confused if both you *and* Lila are chasing him tonight?"

"Why should he be confused? I think he'll be flattered." Jessica did one last twirl before the mirror. "It isn't too late to change what *you're* wearing, you know," she added with a quick, critical glance at Elizabeth's khaki pants and striped tank top.

Elizabeth laughed. "I'm happy as is, Jess. No chance of anyone mistaking us for each other tonight!"

The phone rang as the twins got downstairs. "Let the machine get it, in case it's for Mom," Elizabeth suggested. The machine beeped and they heard Amy Sutton's plaintive voice.

"Jess, where *are* you? I thought we were going to the Beach Disco together tonight. I'll wait at home until seven-thirty, and if I haven't heard from you by then, I'll just go ahead." Elizabeth was about to pick up the receiver, but Jessica stopped her.

"It's almost seven-thirty. Let's just go," Jessica said to Elizabeth.

Elizabeth raised her eyebrows. "Still mad at Amy?"

"Well, I'm not the only one," Jessica retorted. "Didn't I tell you she's been saying she's interested in Tom McKay? Poor Jean is still really upset about him and Amy's acting as if he's hers to pounce on! We *are* all cheerleaders, you know. And cheerleaders should stick together."

Elizabeth groaned as she opened the door. "I don't see why cheerleaders owe each other any more loyalty than any other friends. And as for going after someone else's ex, that's not exactly an abnormal activity in your crowd, is it? I hate to be the one to remind you, Jess, but didn't you try to steal Roger Barrett Patman away from Olivia Davidson a while back? Your crowd doesn't usually require an official mourning period before moving in for the kill!"

Jessica pouted. "I'm surprised you're taking Amy's side. You're the one who always says Amy is flighty and boy-crazy."

"I just think you should be fair, that's all." Elizabeth slipped into the driver's seat of the Fiat. "If you're mad at Amy for something, you should tell her. But I get the feeling you guys are waging a cold war against her. And that isn't very nice."

Jessica was silent for a moment. "Well, maybe we *have* been a little harsh," she admitted. But Jessica wasn't ready to let her friend off the hook so easily. At least, not yet.

By the time Amy pulled up in front of the dance club on the west end of the beach, the parking lot was already crowded. Amy got out of her car and walked slowly toward the building. She wondered if she was dressed right. It was hard coming to this sort of thing all alone without a friend to give her emotional support and wardrobe advice.

Amy had decided to dress all in white. Tom was tennis-obsessed enough to appreciate the look. She had chosen tight white jeans, a white halter top, and a lot of silver jewelry. The Beach Disco often used strobe lights, and Amy thought the effect of the lights on her blond hair and white clothing would be dynamite.

Amy passed inside and looked around for Tom. About fifty kids were already packed onto

61

the small dance floor, and the tables were full as well. It looked like a great party.

Amy narrowed her eyes and scanned the crowd. She spotted Jake right away. He looked very chic in a funky gray jacket, baggy gray trousers, and a wild bow tie. Jessica was hanging on one arm, Lila on the other, Amy noticed. Maybe *that's* why they hadn't answered her phone calls. They were too busy fighting over Enid's cousin!

Enid was sitting at a big table with Elizabeth, Todd, Winston, and a bunch of other kids from school. Amy saw some of the cheerleaders and sorority girls seated at another table. There was Jean West, looking pretty in a blue dress . . . and there was Tom, deep in conversation with her!

Amy quickly pushed her way through the crowded dance floor until she got close to Tom and Jean. She paused and pretended to look around for someone. "Oh, Tom! Jean! Hi," she exclaimed. "Have either of you two seen Jessica?"

It worked. Tom and Jean were forced to interrupt their conversation. Amy stood her ground until they included her in idle chatter. After a few minutes Jean excused herself and vanished through the crowd.

"Tom," Amy said, putting her hand on his arm, "you look *great*. Where on earth did you get that shirt?"

Tom blushed and looked uncomfortable. It was so sweet, Amy thought, his being shy about his appearance!

"I don't remember," he said, looking around nervously.

"Would you like to dance?" Amy asked coyly as a slow song began to play.

"Uh, maybe a little later," Tom stammered.

Amy gave him a warm smile. Tom's answer implied they would be spending a lot of the evening together! She edged closer to him.

"Do you think Jake is having fun?" she asked, nodding toward the spot on the dance floor where Jake was dancing with Enid.

"I hope so. He's a great guy," Tom replied. "And he's an incredible tennis player," Tom continued admiringly.

Amy was glad that Tom was confiding in her. Still, she wanted the conversation to get more personal. "You know, Tom," she said daringly, "I'm not usually this direct, but—"

"Amy, listen, I've got to get something to drink." There was a look of panic on his handsome face. Amy watched in silence as he took off in the direction of the soda machine.

"Problems, Amy?" Lila's face wore a knowing smile. She had come up from behind Amy and had heard Tom's hasty excuse.

Amy felt her face burn. "As a matter of fact, no," she answered. Some friend Lila was, making fun of her about something that really mattered! But then, Lila didn't realize that Tom was not just another crush for Amy. That this time she was really in love.

Amy followed Tom. She refused to give up. She reached the soda machine just as Barry Rork approached from the other direction.

"Hi, Amy!" Barry's eyes brightened. "Want to dance?"

Amy stared at Tom. "Uh, not now, Barry. But thanks anyway," she said. "Tom, won't you let me share that with you? I'm absolutely dying of thirst."

Tom reached in his pocket for two quarters. "Here, take mine. I'll get another one," he said. He would not meet her eyes.

A new song had just begun and Amy tried again. "Ooooh, Tom," she gasped. "This is absolutely my favorite song. Won't you dance with me?"

"Sorry, Amy, but I twisted my ankle slightly today playing tennis. I don't want to risk a serious injury by dancing." Tom was polite but firm.

"I'll dance with you," Barry said. Before Amy could refuse again, he led her onto the dance floor. Amy sighed audibly and watched Tom walk away from the soda machine with evident relief. Now she was stuck dancing with Barry and would probably lose Tom in the crowd. Amy felt her spirits sink. She knew she should be a good sport about dancing with Barry. She did like him a lot. As a friend.

"Barry," she said as he put his arms around her for a slow dance, "can I ask you a huge favor?"

Barry looked as if he were on cloud nine. "Whatever you want, Amy. Just name it."

"Help me get Tom to dance with me," Amy begged.

Barry loosened his embrace a little but said

nothing. Amy didn't lose heart. Barry was her friend, Amy reminded herself. She knew he would help her. He had promised as much the other day, at the clinic.

Jessica wiped her brow and smiled happily. Three dances in a row with Jake! She was having a ball.

"How many for you?" Lila demanded.

Jessica put up three fingers.

"I'm killing you. He's danced five times with me," Lila said triumphantly.

Jessica giggled. "But I got a slow dance. It's quality, Lila, not quantity!"

The girls decided to freshen up. They got in the long line for the girls' bathroom. Across from them, in line for the boys' bathroom, were Tom McKay and Barry Rork, deep in conversation. Jessica's ears pricked up when she heard Amy's name.

"Listen, I'd do anything to be in your shoes," Barry was saying glumly. "But Amy doesn't give me the time of day."

"Tell me what I can do to help. Believe me, I'm not interested," Tom exclaimed.

"Nothing. What can you do? She adores you," Barry said. "All I can do is suffer, I guess."

Tom ran his hand through his hair. "Well, I'm not sure how much longer *I* can suffer. She's been chasing me around all night!"

"Come on, McKay. Don't break my heart," Barry pleaded.

Jessica leaned over to hear more, but the two

boys seemed to sense someone was listening and they fell silent. Jessica looked at Tom and Barry. It did not surprise her one bit that Tom wanted Amy to leave him alone. What *did* surprise her was that Barry Rork sounded totally in love. Jessica knew Barry vaguely through Bruce Patman, another senior on the tennis team. Barry was a nice guy, really sweet and sincere. What could he *possibly* like about Amy Sutton?

As she watched Barry, Jessica remembered a bit more about him. Bruce had said that he was a pretty intense guy, involved in the community, and also a good student. Either Barry had really changed, or he saw something in Amy that nobody else did!

Seven

Tom got to the courts at nine-thirty on Sunday morning. He was supposed to meet Jake at ten, which meant he had half an hour to himself to practice some strokes on the backboard.

Tom quickly got into a rhythm, hitting the ball over and over again. The last few weeks had been very hectic. He had spent a lot of time at tennis practice, and a lot of time with friends. Tom knew he had not really begun to digest what had happened with Jean.

Their having broken up still made him incredibly sad. Tom had never had a steady girlfriend before Jean, plenty of dates, of course, but nothing serious. Jean was one of the nicest girls he had ever met, and he knew he would never forget her. *Never*, he thought, giving the tennis ball a hard swipe with his racket.

Their whole history flashed before him. He remembered, with a pained smile, what Jean had put him through when she had first started to show an interest in him. Jessica Wakefield and some of the other members of Pi Beta Alpha, the sorority Jean had been so eager to join, had made Jean ask him out as part of her pledge task. Tom had been furious when he found out he was being used. But what had started as a dare turned out to be much more. Jean really liked him. A lot. And Tom liked her.

Very quickly they had become boyfriend and girlfriend. Tom had discovered, to his surprise and delight, what wonderful company she was, how understanding, sympathetic, and loving. For a long time they had been very happy together. Then, well, he wasn't sure why, but he had begun to feel as if something important was missing from their relationship.

He still could not understand what had gone wrong between them. Was it just part of growing up, realizing that sometimes relationships didn't make it, and for no apparent reason? Tom had heard guys talking about breaking up with girls. He had heard them say they had gotten bored, that they had met someone new. Well, he didn't have an excuse like that. How could he have gotten bored with Jean? And he certainly could not imagine anyone else he would rather be with. The relationship just hadn't *felt* right, and the more he had tried to hide his feelings, the worse it had become.

Tom sighed, threw his racket up in the air and caught it. The whole thing really hurt, maybe even more because he didn't understand what had happened.

"Hey, Tom! Quit throwing your racket around! You're supposed to be saving your energy for some serious tennis," he heard Jake call.

Tom grinned. It had been great having Jake around this weekend. Jake had helped him take his mind off Jean. In fact, if he were the sort of person who could talk about his feelings, instead of keeping them bottled up inside, he would tell Jake about Jean. Maybe someday he would.

Jake slipped off his tennis sweater and looked closely at Tom. "Were you OK last night? I was worried about you," he said.

Tom smiled self-consciously. "I had to get away for a bit, so I went outside to take a walk."

Jake nodded. "Yeah, I looked for you, and Todd Wilkins told me you'd cut out for a while. Too hot in that place, huh?"

"Well, especially . . ." Tom paused for a second. He was not used to talking about girls, and he did not want to put Amy down, but he would not mind sharing a little of what he had been feeling last night. "You know who Amy Sutton is, don't you? Blond hair, gray eyes? She was wearing all white last night," he added.

Jake nodded. "She's cute," he said neutrally.

"Yeah, well, she may be cute, but she's a little too pushy for my taste." Tom sighed. "I just split up with a girl I'd been seeing for a while. We were pretty serious. But Amy's barely given me a chance to take a breath before jumping all over me!"

"I do remember her following you around. She sure seemed interested." Jake grinned.

"I don't know what it's going to take to get the message that I'm not interested through to her." Tom shook his head. "I had to pretend I needed some air last night, because I couldn't think of any more good reasons not to dance with her!"

"Poor guy," Jake teased. "It's hard having gorgeous girls falling all over you."

Tom laughed. "The worst part of it is that my friend Barry Rork is nuts about Amy, and she won't give him the time of day."

Jake shook his head. "It's rotten, isn't it? Sometimes you feel as if you're always in love with someone who's in love with someone else."

"Yeah," Tom agreed.

Jake hesitated, as if he were going to say something more, then reached for a canister of tennis balls. "But enough talk," he chided. "Let's play some tennis!"

It took both boys a game to warm up. By the third game, Tom was amazed at how well they were both playing. Jake was enough of a better player to make Tom perform at his best. Tom could not believe the shots he was able to make.

"Nice!" Jake called when he won the fourth game.

"Nice for whom?" Tom called back.

But by the middle of the second set, Tom's strength began to serve him well. He won two games in a row, and, with some struggle, was able to take the second set.

"You know, it's lousy having to stop with the

70

sets tied up," Jake said as he wiped his face with a towel. "But I haven't got time for a third set now. I promised Enid I'd meet her back at her house in half an hour."

"How about this afternoon?" Tom asked, still struggling to catch his breath.

Jake shook his head. "I can't, Tom. Enid and I have a lot to catch up on. We've been with her mom and her friends a lot the past few days, and we haven't been able to talk alone."

"How about late this afternoon?" Tom was dying to play the third set.

"I don't really see how. You know Enid's having a party tonight, and I want to help her get things ready." Jake grinned. "Don't look so bummed out. It's great leaving things tied up. That way you can come up to San Francisco sometime to play the last set."

Tom felt funny all of a sudden. It had just struck him that Jake was leaving the next day. "It's too bad you don't live in Sweet Valley," he blurted out.

Jake was leaning over to scoop up his racket. Tom could not see his reaction. "Oh, well," Jake said cheerfully as he stood up. "Just means you'll have a good reason to come up and say hi sometime." He gave Tom a friendly pat on the shoulder and started off toward the parking lot. "You need a ride anywhere?"

"No, thanks," Tom said, watching Jake walk off.

"See you tonight at Enid's, right?" Jake called.

"Right," Tom called back. "Hey, Jake?"

Jake turned and waited.

"Thanks for a great match. A great *almost*-match."

Jake waved his racket. Tom saw him get into Enid's car and pull out of the parking lot.

Tom kicked at the ground with the toe of his tennis shoe. It had been great spending time with Jake Farrell. Tom was really going to miss him.

Amy looked self-consciously around the beach before choosing a spot to spread her towel. She was glad that she didn't see anyone she knew. Amy was used to coming to the beach with a whole group of friends, not slinking around alone hoping no one would guess the truth, that her friends had abandoned her.

It was Sunday afternoon, and Amy wanted to do some suntanning before Enid's party for Jake that evening. She also hoped that some soothing time in the sun would lift her spirits. She was still smarting over what had happened the night before at the Beach Disco. Though she had tried to confront Jessica and Lila about their cold-shoulder treatment, they had still succeeded in putting her off. Proud as she was, Amy knew rejection when she saw it. And the fact that Tom had suddenly needed to take a walk, just when she was giving him one last chance for a dance together . . . well, it had hurt her feelings, all right. But, perversely, Tom's apparent disinterest only strengthened Amy's resolve.

Maybe the old Amy would have given up on Tom after last night, said good riddance and moved on to someone ready to succumb to her considerable charms. But the new Amy was feeling a bit desperate. She was determined to get Tom to like her, no matter how much of a challenge he presented. Amy took out a well-worn copy of *Ingenue* magazine. She wanted to reread the article entitled "How Can You Tell If He's Interested." She had not read far when a shadow crossed the page and a familiar voice said hello.

"Are you all by yourself? Can I sit with you?" Barry Rork asked.

Amy looked up and sighed. A few weeks ago she had barely known Barry. Now she seemed to know him too well.

"Sure," she said, reluctantly rolling up her magazine and slipping it back in her beach bag.

"I decided I needed to get tan. How'm I doing?" Barry demanded.

Amy suppressed a giggle. Barry's skin was fair. But he was not bad-looking, she thought critically. He just needed a little help with choosing more stylish clothes. And a little sun wouldn't hurt him, either. "Maybe you should try taking off your shirt," she suggested.

Barry pretended to be outraged. "Out here? In public?"

Amy laughed. Barry was cute, in a weird sort of way. And it *was* nice that he liked her so much. Not that she would ever be interested in him as anything more than a friend, she assured herself. But she liked his sense of humor, and his company. Maybe her Sunday afternoon wouldn't be so lonely, after all.

"Any chance I'll get another dance tonight, at Enid's?" Barry asked.

Amy was startled. Barry was invited to Enid's? She glanced at him curiously.

"Tom asked me to come with him," Barry explained. "If you don't promise me a dance, I'll feel as if nobody's paying any attention to me." He pretended to gasp melodramatically. "I'll *suffer!*"

Amy pretended to think it over. "I'll give it some serious thought," she teased him. "It'll depend on just how badly you suffer."

It wouldn't be so awful to dance with Barry again. There was always the chance, however slight, that Tom might notice and get jealous.

Tom was mowing the lawn on Sunday afternoon when Jean pulled up at the McKays' curb.

She looked as pretty as ever, he thought admiringly. She was wearing a pink cotton sundress and a little comb held her dark hair back from her face. "Hi, Tom. I hoped you'd be here," she said. She took a shopping bag from the backseat of the car. "I wanted to drop off some things you left at my house," she said softly.

Tom was surprised. "What things?"

"Oh, I had one of your sweaters, one your mom made you. A couple of books, and that radio you loaned me." Jean took a deep breath. "I was cleaning out my room and thought it was a good idea to get it all over with and bring these back, before it gets even harder." Jean's

74

eyes had filled with tears. It was clear how painful it had been for her to return his belongings.

"Jean. . . ." Tom looked hard at her. "Come inside. My parents are out playing golf, there's no one home," he urged. "Come on. I think we should talk."

Jean nodded and followed him inside. Tom felt so strange, sitting next to Jean on the living-room couch, where they had sat so often! Part of Tom wanted to put his arms around her and hug her close, tell her he wanted to try again. But somehow he couldn't bring himself to do it.

Jean wiped her eyes. "The hardest part for me is not understanding why," she said softly. "It's so weird, Tom. When I tell people we've split up, they want to know what happened, and I just don't know what to say. We never had a big fight. We like the same things. We get along so well. . . ." Her eyes brimmed with tears again. Tom felt sick.

"I don't understand it either, Jean. Maybe the answer is that we're not ready for something so serious. I don't know." He shook his head and felt a mixture of relief and sorrow. Why couldn't they be together? *What's wrong with me?* he thought, suddenly hating himself. *Why can't I be in love with her? She's everything I ever wanted. Isn't she?*

"Well," Jean said, fighting hard to keep her composure, "at least we don't hate each other." She tried to smile, but her lips trembled. "We can still be friends, right?" Her eyes were bright, but her voice was heartbreakingly sad.

"Of course!" Tom said. How could he ever

feel anything for Jean but love and respect? He thought she was the nicest girl on earth. To be just friends. . . .

"Tom, do me one favor. Will you hug me, just once? I miss that more than anything, the way your arms feel around me."

Tom nodded. He couldn't talk for the lump in his throat. Jean felt so tiny and fragile in his arms, as if she would break in half if he tightened his embrace. He could feel her heart pounding against his chest. After what felt like a long, long time, Jean pulled back.

"I should go," she whispered. "If I'm ever going to, I should go now."

Tom drew a deep, quavering breath. "OK, then," he whispered. Jean drew away from him and walked slowly to the door.

Tom thought he would never feel as sad as he did that afternoon as he watched Jean drive away. This time, he knew he didn't have another chance. He and Jean were finished. For good.

Eight

Elizabeth went over to Enid's house early on Sunday evening so she could help her friend set up for the party. Enid usually had friends over in tiny groups, and Elizabeth knew that the prospect of a big crowd might be intimidating. But as Enid herself had said, she could hardly *not* invite people who had been so enthusiastic about spending time with Jake, even people such as Lila and Amy, who were not exactly her closest friends!

Mrs. Rollins had suggested that a barbecue would be the easiest way to feed everybody, and when Elizabeth arrived, she and Enid were busily setting out paper plates and napkins on a picnic table and several folding tables in the Rollinses' backyard.

"Where's Jake?" Elizabeth asked as she tore open a package of plastic forks.

"Upstairs taking a shower," Enid answered, avoiding her friend's eyes.

Mrs. Rollins went into the house for a minute, leaving Elizabeth and Enid alone.

"I thought if we brought the stereo speakers out here we could discourage people from going inside more than they have to," Enid said as she busily arranged a cluster of chairs. She still did not look at Elizabeth. She seemed flustered and out of sorts.

Elizabeth knew her friend well enough to guess something was bothering her. "Are you OK, Enid? You look kind of upset."

"I'm fine," Enid said quickly. "Maybe a little tired, that's all. Jake and I were at the beach all afternoon."

Several minutes later Jake appeared, carrying a stack of cassettes. He seemed fairly subdued, and Elizabeth could not help but wonder if Jake and Enid had had an argument.

"I'm sorry this weekend has to end," Elizabeth said at last, to break the silence.

Enid and Jake glanced at each other, then away again. "Me, too," Enid said, a bit unconvincingly.

Elizabeth waited until Jake had gone inside to help Mrs. Rollins before she asked Enid again if everything was OK.

"I can't really talk about it," Enid said quietly. Then, with more resolve, she added, "I promise I'll tell you some other time. But trust me. Everything's OK."

Jake and Mrs. Rollins came back out to the yard. Mrs. Rollins held several bags of potato chips, and Jake hefted a cooler full of cold drinks. Suddenly there was so much to do and so little time that Elizabeth was forced to ignore her friend's trouble. At least until she caught Enid furtively looking at Jake with an expression of wonder and sadness.

"What do you think?" Jessica presented herself to Lila. She had given her tightest pair of blue jeans a new look. "I bleached them. And then I put them on and sat in the bathtub in really hot water," she explained. "I don't think they'll ever come off. So you think Jake will like me in them?"

"You know," Lila replied glumly, falling back on her big bed, "I don't think Jake likes either of us that much, Jess. He's had all weekend to fall madly in love, and it hasn't happened."

Jessica tossed her hair away from her face. "You just don't appreciate subtlety, Lila Fowler. Jake isn't the sort of guy who just pounces on a girl. And tonight's his last night in Sweet Valley. He's bound to make his choice known!"

Lila sighed. "Listen, I think he's a great guy. He's cute, and he has a pretty good sense of humor. But the fact remains that he hasn't really been paying special attention to either one of us. Maybe he *does* have a girlfriend back home. Anyway, I have to confess I don't get the sense he's fallen in love with me. Or with you either, for that matter."

Before Jessica could argue, Lila added, "And nobody could *possibly* fall in love at Enid Rollins's house. They don't even have a swimming pool. Their house is completely unromantic!"

Jessica dabbed on some of Lila's expensive perfume. "Leave it to me, Lila. You can give up if you want to, but I think tonight will be *the* night. And I don't think Jake has a girlfriend back home in San Francisco. He's just playing it cool, waiting for the right moment."

Lila giggled. "Do you think Amy will make as big a fool of herself tonight as she did last night at the Beach Disco?"

"I hope not, for her sake," Jessica said fiercely. "Doesn't she realize Tom's got zero interest in her?"

Lila shrugged. "Apparently not. Do you think we should tell her what you overheard between Tom and Barry last night?"

Jessica shook her head. "Let her find out for herself. She deserves it."

Lila sat up and shrugged her shoulders. "Yeah, I guess. I wouldn't mind a truce, though. I kind of miss Amy."

"Soon," Jessica promised. "After she thrashes around a little bit longer. She's so obsessed with getting Tom that she's probably hardly even noticed we've been avoiding her!"

By eight o'clock Enid's barbecue was in full swing. Music was blasting out over the crowded lawn, guests were talking, eating hamburgers and hot dogs, and dancing on the softly lit patio.

Amy had decided not to come until the party was well under way in order to make an entrance. She had worked hard on her appearance tonight. Betting that everyone else would be wearing jeans, she had chosen a red halter-dress, one that showed off her tan and her figure, and made it hard not to notice her.

Amy headed straight for Enid and Jake to thank them for having invited her. "The party looks like fun," Amy said, craning her neck anxiously. Where was Tom?

She spotted Tom by the grill, trying to balance a plate heaped with food and a soft drink. "Excuse me," Amy said to Enid and Jake as she darted off in Tom's direction.

"Tom! Hi!" she called brightly. Tom didn't acknowledge her greeting, but pushed off through the crowd.

Amy stopped short, disappointed. Someone brushed up beside her. "You look ravishing," Barry announced as he gave her a mock bow.

She looked mournfully after Tom. "Not ravishing enough," she mumbled. Barry followed her gaze and cleared his throat. "Come dance with me," he urged.

"Barry, let's just get some food and sit down for a while. I'm not sure I feel like dancing right now."

She knew her answer was not the most flattering thing she could have said, but it was the truth. And just now, Amy was not up to anything *but* honesty!

*   *   *

"Jake," Jessica said in her most winning flirtatious voice, "do you realize you and I haven't been alone together for a single minute this entire weekend?"

Jake spooned some pasta salad onto his plate. "I've always wondered about that phrase 'alone together.' It doesn't make much sense, does it?" He was teasing. Jessica decided it might be a good sign.

"Well," she continued boldly, "maybe I can show you what it means. Do you want to take a walk?" *What have I got to lose?* she asked herself. After tomorrow she would never see him again, right?

Jake's eyes fixed on hers. "Jessica, I like you a lot. But I'd rather stay here and enjoy being with everyone, OK?"

His rejection was so matter-of-fact that Jessica hardly noticed she had been rebuffed. How had Jake managed to make himself so clear without saying anything hurtful?

"But I'd love to dance," Jake said, smiling warmly.

"Sure." Jessica shrugged. Why not just enjoy Jake's company? After all, Jake was going back to San Francisco the next day. What good would it have done if she *had* swept him off his feet?

Tom was not having a very good time at Enid's barbecue. He was still upset about his talk with Jean earlier that afternoon, and he was finding it almost impossible to avoid Amy Sutton. It seemed that everywhere he turned, there she was, coming toward him with a soda, asking him to dance, making cheerful small talk. He felt like a cornered animal.

"You've got to save me, Barry," Tom whispered to his friend halfway through the evening. "Give her a sedative or something. Knock her out. Just do *something*!"

"I don't know," Barry answered dubiously. "I think she's starting to get the idea."

"Well, *I* don't think so. She must be a glutton for punishment," Tom said woefully.

"I'd do anything to change her feelings, Tom." Barry sighed. "But I can't. I guess you'll have to grin and bear it."

Tom blushed. "Not very sensitive of me, complaining this way," he said. "Sorry, Barry. I know you like Amy. It's just . . ."

Tom stood straighter and took a deep breath. He had noticed Jake, hands deep in his pockets, heading away from the crowd, apparently deep in thought.

"Listen, I'll be back soon," Tom told Barry. Before Barry could answer, Tom hurried after Jake.

"Hey, what are you doing?" Tom called to him when he was a few feet away. "You're not allowed to leave. You're the guest of honor!"

Jake laughed, but he seemed tense. Tom could see the muscles in his jaw tighten.

"I needed a breather. You know how it feels when you've been 'on' all weekend. I thought a quick walk might help me, you know, recharge."

Tom nodded. "Can I come with you? I kind of need to escape, too."

Jake paused and looked at Tom steadily. "OK," he said.

The two boys walked around to the front of Enid's house and onto the sidewalk. Suddenly Tom felt as though there were a million things he wanted to tell Jake. He wished he could tell him about what had happened with Jean, about how upset he was that he didn't know how to handle Amy's advances with a little more skill. He wanted to ask Jake what he thought of Sweet Valley, whether he would ever be back. But instead he walked beside him in silence.

"It's been fun, this weekend," Jake said after a while.

Tom nodded. "Yeah. I've enjoyed having you around." Tom cleared his throat. That was not the sort of thing he usually told his friends, but, well, Tom wasn't sure why, but he felt it was important to tell Jake how he felt.

Jake looked pleased, then slightly ill at ease. "Listen, I'm glad you feel that way. You're a great guy, Tom, you know that?"

Tom reddened. This was so awkward! No wonder guys weren't in the habit of telling each other they valued each other's friendship, the way girls did. It was way too hard! "Thanks. It isn't easy for me to say what I mean sometimes," Tom said, laughing softly.

"It's not always that easy for me, either," Jake agreed. "I often find it hard to connect with people. We don't seem to be on the same wavelength. A lot of people don't like me," he concluded.

Tom looked at Jake with disbelief. "Jake, I

don't believe that. Haven't you seen the way Enid's friends welcomed you? Everyone wants to be with you. Half the girls are in love with you," he added, smiling a bit ruefully as he thought of his own circumstances.

Jake looked distressed, but forced himself to go on. "It's different when you're visiting just for a weekend. People see what they want to. They don't get to know the real me, the me underneath. It's not always easy for me once people find out . . ." Jake's voice trailed off and he stared up at the sky as if he were searching for the rest of his sentence there.

"Find out what?" Tom demanded. What could there possibly be about Jake Farrell that people wouldn't like?

"Once they find out I'm gay," Jake concluded. He didn't look at Tom, but continued to stare at the sky.

Tom stopped. "You're . . . ?"

Maybe he hadn't heard Jake correctly. Jake Farrell? Gay?

"Well, why should that make any difference?" Tom heard himself saying. His voice sounded a little funny, but not shocked. He *felt* shocked, but his voice remained in control.

Jake had continued to walk on a few paces. Now he stopped, turned, and laughed. "I'm glad you feel that way. It's always a little scary, telling people. Especially people you want as friends. Let me tell you, Tom. A lot of people drop you the minute they find out you're gay. Maybe they know what they're doing, maybe they don't. But it hurts the same either way."

Tom nodded. He hoped he looked normal to Jake. His face felt like stone. *Jake Farrell is gay,* he thought.

It doesn't make one bit of difference, he told himself quickly. *Everyone is entitled to whatever lifestyle he or she wants.* That was something Tom had been raised to believe. But right now he felt uncomfortable. Maybe it was hearing Jake's news so directly. All of a sudden, Tom felt very nervous. He felt as though anything he would say would be wrong.

"Well," Tom said at last. He cleared his throat and looked at Jake, as if waiting for some kind of signal.

"Let's head back," Jake said, as if he sensed how awkward Tom was feeling.

Tom nodded. "Fine." He hated himself for the way he felt, but he could hardly wait to get back to the Rollinses' house, to get away from Jake.

Nine

"Enid," Elizabeth said at lunchtime on Tuesday, "are you going to tell me what's bothering you, or do I have to watch you suffer in silence?"

Enid pushed her sandwich away. "I'm upset about Jake," she said simply. "I feel awkward about this, Liz. Jake told me something in confidence and I'm not sure how he'd feel about my telling anyone else."

Elizabeth nodded. A confidence was something she very much respected, and she would never urge her friend to share a secret she had promised not to share.

"On the other hand, I really need to talk it over." Enid brushed back her curly hair in frustration. "I blew it with Jake, big-time. I wouldn't mind getting another perspective on what happened. Particularly from you, Liz. I know you would have done and said the right thing no matter what."

"Tell me what happened," Elizabeth said gently. "I promise no one else will hear about it, not even Todd."

Enid glanced around. "OK, but not here. Let's go outside and sit on the lawn."

"Sure." Elizabeth was a little surprised. Whatever Enid had to say must be pretty serious if she did not want to talk about it in the lunchroom.

"Jake and I spent Sunday afternoon together," Enid said when she and Elizabeth had found an isolated spot on the front lawn. "I had pushed for some time alone with Jake because I got the sense this weekend that he had gone through some big changes. But it was such a social weekend we didn't have any time to really talk until Sunday. At first, the conversation was the usual. Jake wanted to know about boyfriends, and I told him about Hugh. . . ." Hugh Grayson had been Enid's most recent serious boyfriend. "And then he told me about himself."

Elizabeth nodded. "And?"

Enid took a deep breath. "He told me he's gay."

The two girls looked at each other in silence. Elizabeth tried to assimilate the news. "He'd never said anything about it before?" she asked softly.

Enid shook her head. "No. Nothing. To tell you the truth, I was pretty shocked."

"But he must trust you a lot to be able to confide in you," Elizabeth said reassuringly.

Enid looked pained. "Well, that's one of the reasons I feel like such a jerk! Liz, I never thought

I was the slightest bit prejudiced. But when I heard Jake say the word 'gay,' my reaction was terrible! I know I must have looked as if he had just dropped a bomb on me. I couldn't say anything at all for about five minutes. Then I blurted out something dumb like 'Why didn't you tell me before?' as if he'd been keeping a secret from me. Which, of course, he hadn't." Enid looked miserable.

"It's understandable that you'd be startled," Elizabeth said.

Enid shook her head. "Imagine how much courage it took Jake to tell me. The minute I became aware of how I was reacting, I tried to stop myself. All Sunday night at the party I felt like a zombie. I couldn't relax. All I could think about was what Jake had told me, and what kind of an impact it was going to have on *me*." Enid plucked a blade of grass and frowned. "I wonder why reactions to important news tend to be so selfish. I didn't even really think about Jake, about how he must be feeling about my reaction, how hard it must've been for him."

"Well, did you talk to Jake after the party?" Elizabeth asked.

"Yesterday morning, before I took Jake to the airport, we had breakfast together." Enid smiled. "Just the two of us. My mom had gone to the store, and you know, it was like old times! We were goofing around, being silly, he was making me laugh the way he always does. And suddenly I realized that Jake was just—Jake. That what he told me on Sunday doesn't change one thing about him for me. I love him like crazy. It's *who he is* that matters for our relationship, not the kinds of choices he makes about his other relationships."

Elizabeth smiled. "Well, it sounds as if it all worked out. Why are you still upset?"

"Because my first reaction was to be shocked, to judge him. If Jake's own cousin reacted so badly, what can Jake expect from the rest of the world?"

Elizabeth took a deep breath. "You're right," she said. "There are a lot of people out there who will never get past the shock and the judgment. They won't give Jake a chance. They won't ever find out what a great tennis player he is or that he loves jazz and science fiction, that he's a great dancer and a wonderful friend. But, Enid, that's *their* problem!"

"It's Jake's problem, too," Enid said sadly. "I just wish there were some way I could make life easier for him. When we were saying goodbye at the airport, I felt so bad for him, Liz. Not pity. I felt as if I wanted to protect him from all the hurt he's going to have to face."

Elizabeth put her arms around Enid and gave her a warm hug. "I don't think I could have been so honest with myself, that I could have acted with as much love and empathy as you did."

"You would have. Of course you would have," Enid cried. Her eyes filled with tears. "I guess all we've got in the end is our capacity to respect one another," she said softly.

Elizabeth was quiet for a while. "You know," she said at last, "I have a feeling your cousin is going to make it."

"I hope so," Enid said. "It shouldn't have to be so hard for Jake and other people who are gay to make the choice they need to make. There shouldn't have to be so much pain."

Elizabeth didn't know what else to say. She knew there weren't any easy solutions.

"Do you think Jake will come back and visit?" Elizabeth asked her friend.

"Not for a while," Enid said sadly. "But maybe if I keep asking him, he'll come to know how welcome he really is. And that's all I can hope for."

Tom had hardly slept since Enid's barbecue on Sunday night. Each night he lay on his bed and went over his conversation with Jake. Once or twice, early Monday morning, he had picked up the phone to call Jake at Enid's house. But he couldn't bring himself to make the call.

Tom could not understand how he could have let such negative emotions get in the way of his good feelings about Jake. Where had those emotions *come* from? Tom was not a bigot. He didn't have any fixed, narrow ideas about the kinds of private choices people should make. Jake was a wonderful guy, and someone whose friendship Tom had really begun to value. So why had he acted so stupidly when Jake confided in him?

"There must be something wrong with me," Tom muttered as he got dressed for school on Tuesday morning. What possible reason could there have been for the intensity of his reaction on Sunday night . . . unless . . .

Tom suddenly felt cold, even though it was very warm in his bedroom. How had Jake found out he was gay? Did he just wake up one day and know?

Maybe that's why I reacted the way I did, Tom thought. The suddenness of the realization made him sit down on his bed. *Maybe I was so nervous because I'm scared about me. I'm afraid I might be gay, too.*

Tom sat staring out the window. For a while he couldn't bring himself to do anything. He couldn't even bear to put on his shoes and socks or go downstairs for breakfast.

I need to think. Tom ran his hand across his eyes. His relationship with Jeanie had fallen apart because, much as he loved her, he did not, could not feel any passion for her. And what about his feelings toward Amy Sutton? Most guys would be thrilled to have a girl as pretty and as popular as Amy interested in them. Barry, for instance. Barry wanted Amy to like him. And Tom . . . Tom could not imagine anything romantic with Amy at all.

Tom sighed. He felt terrible. What if he *was* gay? Would the kids at school despise or ostracize him? Would he still be able to play on the tennis team? A thousand questions crowded his mind. Tom realized he badly needed to talk to someone. But to whom?

Mr. Collins pushed back his chair and looked thoughtfully at Elizabeth. "See if you can run down to Project Youth sometime this week.

From what Ms. Jacobi tells me about the place, I think it would be a good idea for us to cover it in *The Oracle*," he said. "You might try to get an interview with each of the student volunteers from Sweet Valley High. I think they'd be a real inspiration to the rest of the student body. It takes a lot of courage to work with troubled kids."

Elizabeth nodded. Mr. Collins was her favorite teacher and the faculty adviser for *The Oracle*, Sweet Valley High's school paper.

"Sounds great," she said as she got to her feet. Just then there was a knock on the office door, and Tom McKay stuck his head inside the room.

"Oh, you're busy," he said. He sounded disappointed.

"I'm just leaving, Tom." Elizabeth gave Mr. Collins a wave and slipped out past Tom.

Tom closed the door after Elizabeth. What he had to do was not going to be easy, but of all the people he knew, Mr. Collins was the most sympathetic. Tom had always liked and trusted him.

It took Tom a moment to screw up the courage to begin. When he did start, he told Mr. Collins what had happened with Jake on Sunday night, and about how upset he had been over his reaction to Jake's telling him he was gay.

"I feel like such an idiot. Jake was really taking a risk, trusting me, and what did I do? I know I made him feel awful," Tom said.

Mr. Collins nodded. "Tom, sexuality isn't an easy subject for people of any age. But for people of your age, it's the very hardest. It's not at all unusual for teenagers to question their sexual identity and to feel uncomfortable talking about it with another person."

Tom took a deep breath. "I'm sort of wondering about myself," he blurted out.

Mr. Collins was silent. His frank, sympathetic expression made it easier for Tom to go on.

"I'm scared to talk about it, but I feel as if I need advice," he said.

Mr. Collins nodded. "I don't blame you. You must feel very much alone and very confused." He reached for a piece of paper and wrote something on it. "There's a clinic in town that runs support groups for teenagers. I think the director may be able to help place you in one. Why don't you call her and make an appointment?" When Tom hesitated he added, "It's confidential, of course."

"I'm not ashamed," Tom said quickly. "I'm just confused."

Mr. Collins smiled. "I understand, Tom. And I'm glad you could talk to me. So often it's easier to keep something inside than to open up about it."

Tom took a deep breath. "I think I'm beginning to realize that."

"And maybe someday you can let Jake know how much his confidence meant to you," Mr. Collins added.

Tom nodded. One day soon, he would write

Jake and thank him. He was still deeply ashamed of the way he had treated Enid's cousin. But at least now he was able to see some of the reasons for his own reaction.

However hard it would be, it was time to start figuring out who Tom McKay really was.

Ten

Elizabeth enjoyed her interview with Kathy Henry. She found the young director of Project Youth to be enthusiastic and forthright about the clinic and its goals. "We hope to fill a need in the community," Kathy told her as they wrapped up the interview. "Sweet Valley is a wonderful town, but that doesn't mean its teenagers don't need people to talk to when they're in trouble. And Project Youth also serves as a network to other clinics in the area." She grinned. "Right now, what we need most of all is publicity. I'm glad you're doing this story in your school paper. It will help to get the word out."

Elizabeth shook Kathy's hand and promised to send her a copy of the article when it was published.

"One last thing. I was hoping to do interviews with the student volunteers from Sweet Valley High," Elizabeth said.

Kathy glanced at her schedule. "Neither of the students is here this afternoon, but I can tell you, they're both terrific. You know, our high school volunteer program is relatively new, and I think when other kids hear their stories, they'll be interested in joining us. Why don't I give you their names so that you can arrange to interview them at school?"

"That's fine."

"Here, let me write them down for you." Kathy reached for a pencil and paper. "Barry Rork has been with us for over a year. He's a tremendous asset to the clinic and we're hoping he'll train to be a full counselor. The other volunteer has just started, but she's proving to be every bit as good. Her name is Amy Sutton."

Elizabeth was not sure she had heard Kathy correctly. "Amy—" she began.

"Amy Sutton. I think she's a junior," Kathy said as she handed Elizabeth the slip of paper.

Who would have guessed, Elizabeth thought, that Amy Sutton would *volunteer* for anything! Let alone for a worthwhile project like the youth clinic! Even more astonishing to Elizabeth was the fact that she had won the respect of the clinic's director. Pretty impressive for a girl who appeared to be such a flake, Elizabeth thought admiringly. "Thanks, Kathy. I'll find Barry and Amy at school and get the inside story on being a student volunteer."

"Great. You can go out through the waiting area." Kathy pointed ahead. "I have to visit our volunteers on the phone lines."

Elizabeth walked through the small, comfortably furnished waiting area. She was so absorbed with all the things Kathy Henry had told her about the clinic that she almost didn't realize the boy sitting alone in the room was Tom McKay. Tom had not noticed Elizabeth because he was intently reading a pamphlet.

Elizabeth opened her mouth to say hello, then closed it. What if—

Tom folded the pamphlet and stood up to slip it into the metal rack on the wall. As he stood he saw Elizabeth. Her eyes automatically flicked to the title of the pamphlet Tom held, "Teens and Homosexuality," and then to Tom's face. He was bright scarlet.

"Tom, hi," Elizabeth said quietly.

"Hi," he mumbled. He stared at the carpet for a moment and then returned to his seat.

Elizabeth took a deep breath and sat down on the chair next to Tom's. She felt as if she had to say something to ease his discomfort. "Listen, I didn't mean to barge in on you," she said. "I was here interviewing Kathy Henry." She cleared her throat awkwardly.

"I guess I'm going to have to get used to stuff like this." Tom smiled feebly.

Elizabeth glanced at the pamphlet that was now sitting in the rack. A million thoughts rushed through her mind, but she didn't say a word. She waited to hear what Tom had to say.

"I feel as if I don't know who I am anymore," Tom said sadly. He propped his head on his hands and leaned forward. "If you'd told me a couple of months ago that I'd be in a place like this, thinking . . . thinking the kinds of things I've been thinking . . ."

Elizabeth wondered if Tom had found out about Jake's being gay. Was that what had triggered his own questioning?

"Liz, can I ask you a question?" Tom said suddenly.

"Sure, Tom."

"If you . . . let's say you found out something about yourself that was kind of surprising. The kind of thing you know a lot of people wouldn't like. Would you tell people, or would you keep it a secret?"

Elizabeth thought seriously before answering. She knew Tom was asking a difficult question. She remembered what Enid had said about Jake having to face prejudice in his life. Elizabeth realized that Tom's choice was not an easy one. Some people would just not want to accept the truth. Still, he couldn't pretend to be something he wasn't.

"I can only tell you what I'd do," Elizabeth said slowly. "This might not be right for everyone. But I would need to tell the people closest to me, my best friends, my family. Other people . . ." She shrugged. "I guess I'd try as hard as I could just to be myself. If the other people didn't want to accept the real me, then they wouldn't be worth my time."

Tom nodded. "You're probably right, Liz."

Elizabeth felt a wave of empathy and admiration wash over her. What lay ahead for Tom was not going to be easy. She just hoped his friends would stick by him.

"Tom, thanks for talking to me," she said softly as she put her hand on his arm.

99

He nodded. "But, Liz, listen. Don't say anything to anyone yet, OK? Please don't tell anyone you saw me here. I need to do this my own way, at my own speed."

"I won't tell a soul," Elizabeth promised.

Kathy Henry stepped into the waiting area. "Tom? Come on back," she said cheerfully.

Elizabeth watched Tom leave with Kathy. Kathy would be sure to give Tom sound advice; she would know how best to help him as he tried to sort things out. *Kathy wasn't kidding when she said this clinic fills a real need*, Elizabeth thought as she left Project Youth.

It was hard to sort out exactly how she felt about her conversation with Tom. She knew she was glad Tom had someone he could turn to. But she could not help but feel a little apprehensive.

If Tom did confide in his friends, would the students at Sweet Valley High come through for Tom? Would they be supportive and understanding, or would they make him regret ever having trusted them?

Tom was surprised by how much better he felt after his conversation with Kathy Henry. He had expected to come away from the session feeling like a "patient," like someone who was sick. Kathy had quickly changed his mind about that.

"Try not to think in terms of labels," she advised him. "You're at an age when labels are too easy to throw around. You're still unformed, still in transition. I'd also like you to try not to think in terms of 'crises' or 'problems.' You're not sick or in trouble, Tom. You've got some big questions and some important exploration before you. Try not to judge yourself. And above all, watch out for labels!"

So the important thing right now isn't to rush to decide whether or not I'm gay, Tom thought. Kathy had signed him up for a support group she thought would benefit him. "And talk to your friends," she advised him. "They'll help, a lot. And the ones who don't help weren't really friends in the first place."

Tom got on his bike and set off in the direction of school. He was supposed to meet Barry in twenty minutes, and he didn't want to be late. "The ones who don't help weren't really friends." Was that what Jake was thinking right now about Tom? That he wasn't much of a friend?

He couldn't blame Jake if he *was* thinking that. *What a selfish jerk I was*, Tom thought unhappily. Instead of listening to Jake, instead of trying to put himself in Jake's place and imagine how he felt, he had only thought about himself.

Barry was waiting for Tom at the courts.

"Something tells me today's my day. I'm not going to let you cream me the way you usually do," Barry told him. It was a typical, cheerful comment, but Barry's voice sounded a little forced.

Tom laughed. "I'm sure you're right. Judging from the kind of day it's been, you'll probably take every game away from me."

The two played in silence for a while. By the second set, Tom was actually starting to relax and to enjoy himself. Barry, he noticed, was unusually subdued.

"You doing OK?" Tom asked him when they took a quick break.

"Yeah, I guess." Barry sighed. "I'm a little bummed out about this thing with Amy. I know it's dumb, but I really like her a lot."

Tom was quiet for a minute. He remembered what Jake had said, that sometimes it seemed as though everybody was in love with the wrong person. "Listen, have you tried telling her how you feel?" he asked.

Barry wiped his brow with a towel. "Tom, tell me the honest truth. You're not interested in her? Not at all?"

Tom laughed. "No, Barry. I promise. Not one bit."

"Really?" Barry's face brightened a little. "And you wouldn't mind if I told her how much I like her? See, I've been afraid to bring this up, because I thought, well, you know, that you just weren't interested in Amy *right now*, because of Jean. Once you're over Jean, I thought you might want, you know. . . ."

Tom couldn't believe his ears. Barry had been afraid to ask him about Amy. Suddenly it seemed so crazy to Tom how scared people were to admit their real feelings. "Listen, Barry," he said, almost before he realized what he was saying, "I'm not sure I'm interested in girls, period."

Barry stared at him. "Are you . . ." He broke off.

102

"I don't know, Barry. I just don't really know."
Tom took a deep breath. "I'm telling you this
because you're a good friend. I keep trying to
figure out why things didn't work out with
Jeanie. She's a fantastic girl. For a while I thought
she was everything I ever wanted. But the relationship didn't hold together, for reasons I'm
just beginning to understand."

"This is serious stuff, Tom," Barry said.

"Yeah, it is. But—" Tom remembered Kathy's
warning. "But I don't expect a final answer
anytime soon. All I'm saying is, don't worry
about me and Amy, OK?" He tapped Barry on
the arm with his racket. "Do yourself a favor
and tell her how you feel. You'll never forgive
yourself if you don't."

Barry nodded. "You're right." He waited a
minute before speaking again. "Thanks for the
advice. You're a pretty perceptive guy."

"And you're about to lose the last set unless
you concentrate on the game," Tom joked.

Tom was glad he had been able to tell Barry
what he was thinking. Barry had not reacted as
if Tom had made a horrifying confession or
revealed a terrible dark secret. Maybe he had
not said everything he had wanted to, but more
confidences would come with time.

Barry had not run away from Tom or treated
him like a monster. As he took his place on the
other side of the net he seemed every bit at ease
with Tom as he had before. Enough at ease to
fling his racket to the ground when Tom trounced
him, two sets to one.

*　　*　　*

Jessica went to Lila's house after school on Wednesday afternoon to rehash the weekend. It had been harder than she had guessed to say goodbye to Jake, to accept the fact that nothing romantic was ever going to happen between them.

"I still think Jake's the cutest guy to have visited Sweet Valley in ages. If only he lived a little closer, I'm sure he'd come around," Jessica said thoughtfully as she thumbed through the latest issue of *Ingenue* magazine.

"I don't know about that. Persistence doesn't always pay off," Lila reminded her. "Look at Amy. She's only making things worse by pursuing Tom, and she doesn't even realize it."

"Lila, I hope you're not suggesting I'd ever be as crude as Amy's being," Jessica said. She was horrified. "I don't blame Tom for being scared off. Amy's just *chasing* him now. She could at least try to be a little more subtle," Jessica added.

"Yeah. She should have tried to make him jealous," Lila said slowly.

"Maybe. If I were her, I would have been really sympathetic about the breakup with Jean. You know, play the role of supportive friend for a while," Jessica mused. "*Then*, once he really trusted me, I would have pounced. But not before."

"You know, Amy really needs us. She can't help it if she's simpleminded sometimes," Lila declared nobly.

Jessica frowned. "I don't think she deserves help, to tell you the truth."

"Well, I'm not sure our help would make any difference now. I think she's ruined her chances with Tom all on her own," Lila said. "But I do think Amy deserves a break. After all, she *has* been deprived of our wonderful company for over a week!"

"True," Jessica conceded. She had to admit she was beginning to miss Amy Sutton, just a little. "All right, I'll tell you what. After one more day of the silent treatment we'll give her another chance."

"Great idea!" Lila bounced off her bed. Her eyes sparkled. "I can't wait to hear Amy's version of her disastrous romance!"

Jessica groaned. One thing she had no illusions about was Amy's personal version of her pursuit of Tom McKay. Still, Jessica was a little curious to hear how Amy was handling this most recent spectacular rejection.

No doubt she would come crawling back to her friends, Jessica thought with pleasure. She would admit how silly she had been. And then Jessica and Lila would have the pleasure of telling Amy that they had told her so!

Eleven

Amy wandered into her parents' bedroom. It was the middle of the week already, Wednesday night. It had been a long and tiring day, and she had been hoping for a chance to talk to her mother alone. But so far, that hadn't happened.

"Sweetie, I've been so busy lately," her mother said, giving Amy a quick kiss as she scooped up some papers from her bedside table. "I've never seen things at the station this busy. And your father's been working like a maniac on his book." She looked at Amy and smiled sadly. "You must feel as if we've abandoned you."

Amy sighed. "That's OK, Mom. But I did want to ask for some advice. If you've got a minute."

"Of course I've got a minute!" her mother said, glancing quickly at the memo.

Amy took a deep breath. "What would you

do if there was someone you really, really liked
. . . I mean, not just a crush, but someone po-
tentially *serious*?"

Her mother smiled. "What do you mean, what
would I *do*? Do you have to *do* something?"

"Well, in this case, yes," Amy said unhappily. "I'm not sure he feels the same way as I
do. He recently broke up with a girl. Maybe he
just needs more time to get over her," she added.

Mrs. Sutton paid closer attention when she
saw how distressed her daughter looked. "Is
this someone at school?"

"You don't know him, but, yeah, he's a junior. He's a wonderful guy, Mom." Amy's eyes
shone. "He's a great tennis player, and he's
incredibly cute."

Mrs. Sutton raised her eyebrows. "But what's
he like, Amy?"

Amy stared at her mother uncomprehendingly.
Hadn't she just told her mother what Tom was
like? "What do you mean? He's got blond hair,"
she said. "He's, I guess he's sort of a jock, if
you know what I mean."

Mrs. Sutton laughed. "I'm not sure I do.
You're not in love with someone just because
he has blond hair and plays tennis, are you?
Amy, what's his personality like? His character?"

Amy was surprised. She hadn't really thought
much about Tom's personality. "He's popular,"
she began. "Kids at school like him a lot.
He's . . ." Amy suddenly realized that she really
didn't know Tom all that well. What *was* he like?
Amy blushed. "You know, like I said before. Not
just a jock. And popular, too."

Mrs. Sutton shook her head. "I don't think your labeling Tom as a jock or popular is going to help this relationship one bit, Amy. How do you suppose Tom would describe *you*?"

The question astonished her. How would Tom describe *her*? Hopefully, he would say she was pretty. Even beautiful. And popular. *Or at least I was popular before my best friends abandoned me,* she thought sadly.

Amy felt a bit unsteady. Cute and popular. That could be almost any girl at Sweet Valley High!

"My advice would be to get to *know* him," Mrs. Sutton said. "Become his friend. Sometimes a good friendship leads to a good romantic relationship." Mrs. Sutton gave her daughter an affectionate hug. "And if something romantic doesn't happen, at least you've got a new friend!"

Amy thought suddenly about Barry. Now, she could describe Barry's personality in a second! Funny, a little weird, very sensitive and caring, intelligent. But that was different. That wasn't the stuff of a romantic hero.

Was it?

Amy blinked. *I must be losing my mind,* she thought. She shook her head as if to clear it. What on earth would her friends say if she ever went out with someone like Barry?

"I think I just need to try harder," she mused, half to herself, half to her mother. "Mom, what do you think about girls asking guys out?"

Her mother laughed. "You're asking a woman sportscaster about traditional gender roles? Amy, didn't I ever tell you that I asked your father out on our first date?"

Amy's eyes brightened. Now, this was the kind of information she wanted to hear!

"So if I did something like invite him to a concert, you think it would be OK?"

"Why not?" Mrs. Sutton smiled. "The worst that could happen is that he'd say no. But chances are that he'd be thrilled."

A shadow of doubt crossed Amy's mind. *Would* Tom be thrilled? She wished she could be sure!

"What do you have available for Saturday?" Amy asked the young woman in the ticket booth. It was Thursday afternoon, still early enough to get tickets for a great show this weekend. A show Tom could not say no to.

"Well, let's see." The woman studied her computer screen. "I've got two seats left for the Number One concert." The Number One was one of the most popular bands in California.

"Great!" she exclaimed. "How much are they?"

"They're very good seats. The tickets are thirty dollars each," the woman replied.

Amy couldn't believe it. Sixty dollars for two tickets?

"What else is on?" she asked uncertainly.

"Not much. Oh, there's a folk festival at the Civic Center," the woman replied.

Amy dug out her wallet. "I'll take the tickets for the Number One," she said. She couldn't believe she was spending so much money, but she had no idea whether Tom would enjoy the folk festival. *Now at least I know he'll want to go. Who wouldn't, with great tickets like these?* she reasoned.

Amy turned away from the counter and slipped the two tickets into her wallet. She heard someone call her name. Barry Rork was crossing the street, a big smile on his face.

"Amy, hi! I didn't think I'd run into you. Are you going to the clinic?"

Amy nodded. "Yeah. I had to buy some tickets first."

Amy fell into step beside him.

"What tickets?" he asked her.

"I got two tickets to hear the Number One this Saturday night. Center aisle, four rows back," she said, grinning triumphantly. "Barry, I'm going to ask Tom to go with me. Do you think he'll be up for it?" Amy had not intended to tell Barry about her plan, but she was so excited she had to tell someone. Besides, she trusted Barry's opinion as one of Tom's good friends.

A frown crossed Barry's face. Barry stopped and looked straight at her. "Can I tell you what I really think? You won't get upset?"

Amy stared back. "You can say whatever you want to," she answered, a little defensively.

"I don't think Tom's going to want to go to the concert," Barry said simply.

"How do you know?" Amy's voice shook slightly.

"I just . . . well, it's just this feeling I have," Barry answered somewhat weakly.

"You're just saying that," Amy snapped. "You don't have any reason for thinking he won't go."

"Trust me, Amy. He's not interested," Barry said bluntly. "I wouldn't say this if I didn't . . . if I weren't your friend."

"Thanks a lot for the information," Amy said coldly.

"Amy, please don't be angry at me," Barry pleaded, reaching for her hand.

Amy snatched it away. Still, she tried her best not to let Barry see how really upset she was. Had Tom said something to Barry about her? Her face red and her eyes flashing, Amy marched ahead of Barry until they reached the clinic. She had another training session, then joined him at the phones. For the rest of the afternoon she ignored him. And when he asked if he could take her out for a soda after work, she spat out the words "No thanks."

Amy had planned to ask Tom to the concert sometime before lunch on Friday. But she never got the chance. She was going to have to wait until lunchtime.

Much to Amy's surprise, Jessica and Lila approached her as she sat at a table by herself.

"Can we sit here?" Jessica asked.

Lila put her tray down before Amy could say a word. "We've been wondering about you. How's it going with Tom?" she asked, giving Jessica a sly look.

Amy looked from one to the other. "Fine," she said coolly.

111

"Yeah? He didn't look as if he was really all that interested last weekend," Jessica commented.

"In fact," Amy said, ignoring Jessica's remark, "I'm taking him to the Number One concert on Saturday night." Again, Amy had not meant to tell anyone about her plan. But seeing her friends' awed faces, she thought she had done the right thing.

Jessica looked impressed. "You're kidding. You got tickets to the concert? Who did you bribe?"

"And Tom's going with you?" Lila demanded.

"Well . . ." Amy couldn't exactly lie. "He hasn't said yes yet."

"Ah ha!" Lila cried.

"Because I haven't asked him yet," Amy continued. "But I'm going to. In fact, I was planning to ask him at lunch, but then you guys came over." Amy frowned at her friends.

"Well, why should we stop you?" Lila suggested.

Amy blushed. "I don't want to ask him in front of a lot of people. It might embarrass him." She fiddled with her napkin.

"It won't embarrass him," Lila insisted. "Look, there he is."

Tom McKay and several members of the tennis team, including Barry Rork and Kirk Anderson, were heading toward a nearby table. Lila waved them over. "Come over here, guys. We've got lots of room," she called brightly.

Tom looked anxiously at Amy and glanced at his friends who were already pulling extra chairs up to the table. "Uh, OK," he mumbled.

Jessica poked Amy under the table. "Go on," she hissed. "Ask him."

Amy cringed. This was not the setting she had had in mind, but she seemed to have no choice. She might not be able to get Tom alone at all after lunch. "Tom, I was looking for you," Amy said coyly.

"Really?"

"I've been dying to tell you about my surprise for Saturday night. I managed to get fourth-row seats for the Number One concert at the Atrium!"

Tom looked at his food. His face turned slightly pink.

"And I wondered if you would go with me," Amy added quickly.

Tom picked up his sandwich. "I don't think so, Amy. But thanks, anyway."

Lila gave Amy a jab under the table and Amy felt her cheeks burn. She had never been so humiliated. This could not be happening. Lila and Jessica would never let her live this down! They would tell everyone she was a complete jerk. They would tease her, probably even kick her out of the sorority for being such a drip.

"Tom, you have to." Amy could not believe she was begging.

"I, uh, Amy, I can't," Tom said again. "I'm sorry."

Amy could feel Barry's compassionate gaze on her. It made her feel even worse than Jessica's and Lila's amused smirks.

"Oh, don't be such a killjoy," she said to Tom lightly, but a little pleadingly as well. "You

113

can't miss the best concert of the year. They've got a great group opening for them, too."

Kirk Anderson rolled his eyes. "Tom, I think you're going to have to spell it out for her. N O means no. You know, Amy's not exactly a rocket scientist." He laughed meanly. "What else can you expect from a dumb blonde."

"Cut it out, Anderson," Barry said angrily.

Amy felt tears sting her eyes. Never in her whole life had anyone said anything that insulting about her. What made it worse was that he had said it right to her face, as if she had absolutely no feelings. Amy felt as if she had been slapped. Dumb blonde! How could Kirk have called her that?

"I've got to go," she said. She could feel herself trembling as she got to her feet.

"Amy, wait," Tom said.

"Don't listen to Kirk. He's a fool," Barry added.

Even Lila and Jessica looked sympathetic. But Amy refused to listen. She had had it, with every single one of them. Some friends, she thought miserably. Jessica and Lila had actually enjoyed watching Tom make a fool of her.

Amy knew exactly how little everyone thought of her. And that being the case, she was much better off alone!

Well, forget them. Amy stormed out of the lunchroom and raced to the library. She could be sure neither Jessica nor Lila would follow her there. As for Tom, she was never going to speak to him again.

Twelve

The rest of the day was a blur. Amy tried to block out the memory of the humiliating scene at lunch, but it refused to stay hidden. Jessica and Lila would never let her live it down. She could just imagine what the two of them were saying about her right now. And Tom and Barry . . .

Amy couldn't help but remember what her mother had asked her. How *would* Tom describe her? As a dumb blonde, Amy thought, furious tears springing into her eyes. Someone too stupid to understand when she was being rejected.

What a jerk I've been. Amy sighed. She walked to her locker to put her books away after the final bell.

An envelope was taped to her locker door. "For Amy," it said. Inside was a note from Tom.

Dear Amy,

I'm really sorry I can't go to the concert with you this weekend. I'm going through a hard time right now and I don't think I'd be very good company. But thanks for asking me.

Barry and I took care of Kirk. He's an idiot sometimes! Don't pay any attention to what he said, OK?

Tom

Amy bit her lip. That was nice of him, she conceded. He didn't have to write her an apology letter. Maybe, just maybe, the fact that he wasn't interested in her romantically right now didn't mean he didn't like her as a person. Maybe he *didn't* think she was a dumb blonde, after all.

But the rest of them, Jessica, Lila, and Barry. They were still laughing at her. She just knew it.

"Amy, wait up!" a breathless voice cried. It was Jessica, her face red from running down the hall.

"Where have you been? I've been looking for you all afternoon," Jessica panted.

Amy looked at her suspiciously. "I've been around."

"Listen, I just wanted to tell you I think Kirk Anderson is a creep. He never should have said what he did at lunch."

"You do?" Amy could barely believe her ears.

"Yeah, I do. And I bet Tom would've gone to the concert with you if he weren't still upset about Jeanie," Jessica added generously.

116

Amy's heart pounded. Jessica, making excuses for her? She hadn't expected this.

"I'm not so sure," Amy admitted. "I don't think he's very interested in me."

Jessica shrugged. "His loss, then. Right?" She gave Amy one of her most winning smiles, and for a second Amy felt a little bit better.

"I must've looked like such a fool," Amy moaned as the memory of the fiasco came flooding back in all its vivid horror.

Jessica's turquoise eyes were thoughtful. "I wouldn't worry too much about it. Just forget the whole thing," she advised. "Anyway, Anderson is hardly the one to call someone *dumb*." Jessica laughed. "I heard he flunked three of his classes last term."

Amy smiled. Maybe her friends were not so bad after all.

"And there's certainly nothing wrong with being blond," Jessica pointed out.

"I bet everyone at the whole table talked about it when I left," Amy continued, hoping to hear the gruesome truth now and get it over with.

"Unh-unh," Jessica denied. "Barry really laid into Kirk, though. That guy adores you," she declared.

"Barry?" Amy laughed uncomfortably. "Just my luck to have a guy like that adore me." So Barry had defended her, too, she thought. He could have laughed and gone along with Kirk. But no. She was being unfair to him. Barry had never been anything but a good friend to her.

Jessica shrugged. "I think Barry's pretty cute. And he's really funny, too."

Amy was surprised. She thought Jessica would snub Barry in a second. Had she so misjudged him? And Jessica? A warm feeling came over her as she imagined Barry defending her.

"Where are you going now?" Jessica asked as Amy spun her locker dial shut.

"I've been volunteering two days a week at the youth clinic downtown," Amy told her. "I thought I'd head down there and see what's going on."

Jessica's eyes widened. "What kind of clinic? What do you do? I didn't know you had a job!"

Amy shrugged. "It's nothing, really. I've been doing it as an extra-credit project for sociology. I've been working on the phone lines. Teenagers call in and I listen to them. Sometimes I give them advice."

"Sounds like my kind of job," Jessica joked. "Lots of phone time."

"Actually," Amy said, "the work is pretty hard. Lots of the kids who call in have serious problems. Some just want to talk, some are just lonely. But I really like the work. I may even stay on once my project's finished." Amy waited for Jessica's reaction. She couldn't believe she was talking this way to Jessica. She had thought she would keep her work at the clinic a secret to avoid being teased about it.

"That sounds great," Jessica said, looking both impressed and surprised. "Wow, Amy, I'd never have guessed you'd be into something like social work."

Neither would I, Amy thought.

"So I guess that means you don't really feel like going to the mall," Jessica continued.

Amy smiled. "How about picking me up at the clinic in an hour?" Enjoying her work at the clinic didn't mean giving up shopping! And it had been a long time since she had been to the mall with her friends!

"Great. I'll see if Lila wants to come, too." Jessica bounded off with a final wave. Amy watched her, a smile playing about her lips.

Amy got back from the mall just before dinner. Her parents were on the patio, drinking iced tea.

"Amy! Your father finished the new draft of his book. We want to go out to dinner to celebrate," her mother said, beaming.

Amy looked at them uncertainly. Did her mother mean just the two of them, or was she included?

"You've been so patient with me, both of you." Her father grinned. "The least I can do is treat my two favorite women to a lovely dinner."

Amy was relieved. "That sounds great," she said. "I can wear the new sweater I just bought at the mall."

Her mother laughed. "You know, we've been feeling pretty badly about how little time we've been spending as a family lately," she said. "In fact, I talked to my staff today. I'm making it a rule to be home earlier from now on. And no more taking on assignments I could just as easily give to my assistants."

Mr. Sutton nodded. "We don't want to drift apart, just because we're all busy."

Amy looked from one parent to the other. "So I wasn't just imagining it?"

"I think we've been fairly preoccupied," her mother said.

Amy took a deep breath. "That isn't the only thing," she blurted. "Sometimes you two act as if you don't take me seriously. Just because I'm young and I haven't found anything I'm intense about yet, like you're intense about your careers." Amy couldn't look either of them in the eye. She had never planned to say that to them.

"Amy, what do you mean?" her mother asked softly.

"I just want to feel . . . I don't know. I want to know that you two respect me," Amy said.

Her father stood up and put his arm around her. "Sweetheart, we do respect you. Your mother and I can get too wrapped up in our work. We think it's delightful you're not as stressed out as we are!"

"Please don't just say that if you don't mean it," Amy pleaded.

"Amy, we do mean it," her mother said. "Your father and I both believe that what matters most in life is to be *happy*. And it takes time and concentration to discover what you like to do. When I spoke to you last week about your plans for college, I wasn't trying to force you to make a decision based on what your father or I decided for ourselves years ago. We want you to care about what you choose to do with your life, but what counts most is that *you* choose it."

Amy smiled. Her parents sounded as if they really meant what they said. She took a deep breath and nodded. "OK," she said. "I think I'm ready for some celebrating now!"

"Great!"

"Oh, by the way, Amy, I took a message for you from Elizabeth Wakefield. She's doing a story on a local youth clinic for the school paper." Mrs. Sutton looked curiously at her daughter. "Something about student volunteers. Do you know what she's talking about?"

Amy turned pink. Elizabeth Wakefield wanted to do an interview with her?

"Oh, it's nothing," she said quickly. "I've been doing some volunteer work at Project Youth two afternoons a week."

"What do you mean, 'nothing'? Why didn't you mention it before?" her mother asked, surprised.

"Well, to tell you the truth . . ." Amy sighed. "I started out doing it to raise my sociology grade. My work there certainly didn't seem like anything to brag about! But I found I really like working at the clinic, and I think I may keep on even after I've finished the report I'm writing for my teacher."

"Exactly what kind of clinic is it?" her father asked. He seemed really interested.

Amy described Project Youth and told her parents a little bit about what it was like to take calls from troubled kids. They listened avidly.

"Amy, it sounds very exciting," her mother exclaimed.

"Yeah? Do you think I might be a good social worker one day?" she asked uncertainly.

121

Mr. Sutton gave her a hug. "Well, that's something you'll be the best judge of. But I'd bet any amount of money on it. I know that whatever you choose to do, you'll do well!"

"So you guys don't think I'm a dumb blonde?" Amy asked.

"What?" her mother cried.

"Did someone call you that?" her father demanded.

"Just some jerk at school," Amy muttered.

Her mother's expression was furious. "I can't stand it when people put each other down that way! Especially after women have worked so hard to have the same legal rights that men have enjoyed for years. . . ."

Amy swallowed hard. Deep down she knew that Kirk Anderson was not the only one guilty of stereotyping. Hadn't she done more or less the same thing to Tom? A "cute blond jock," that's what she had called him.

It wasn't just guys who labeled girls, she realized unhappily. Sometimes girls were just as guilty as guys.

Maybe now that she knew she had the support of her friends and family she could learn to start thinking about guys more fairly. After all, they were people, too!

"Hey, all this talk has made me hungry. Any chance we can get some dinner?" her father asked.

Amy was just going inside to change into her new sweater when the doorbell rang. Her mother, who had followed her in, went to answer it.

"Flowers?" her mother said wonderingly as she admired the sweet, bright blooms. "These are gorgeous. I wonder who they're from? Maybe Gwynn from the station sent these, in celebration of the Stan Maverick interview."

"Hey, they could be for me," Mr. Sutton called as he came from the back of the house. "A subtle hint from my editor!"

"They're for Amy!" Mrs. Sutton exclaimed as she read the envelope attached to the bouquet.

Amy's eyes grew wide. She had never received a bouquet before, delivered from the florist. The flowers were gorgeous. She closed her eyes and took a deep, appreciative sniff.

"Who are they from?" her mother asked excitedly.

Amy slipped the card out of the little envelope. "I hope these brighten your weekend. Lots of love, Barry," she read aloud.

A blush spread across her face.

"Uh-oh," her father said, grinning. "Looks like my daughter has a real fan."

"Amy, are these flowers from that boy you were telling me about the other night? The one you like so much?" her mother asked.

Amy started to say no, then stopped and shook her head. "They're from a friend," she said mysteriously. She slipped off to the kitchen to put the flowers in water.

Barry was a pretty special guy. Maybe Jessica was right. He wasn't so bad-looking. Not bad-looking at all. And he sure knew how to lift her spirits!

*　　*　　*

123

"Nothing like a Saturday afternoon," Lila crooned. She lay flat on her back on the hot sand, her eyes squeezed shut. "Am I tan yet?"

Amy giggled. "We just got here, Lila."

Jessica was sitting up, her eyes fixed on the spot where some surfers were getting ready to test the waves. "Look at those muscles. Those guys are gorgeous," she exclaimed.

Amy followed her gaze. They *were* handsome. She felt a brief pang of regret as she thought about how she had admired Tom's muscular build.

But Amy had to admit it was not *Tom* she missed. She had never really known him as a person. She had loved the way he looked, she had loved his image. That's all she had been pursuing—an image, and not a real person. And one of the lessons Amy had learned was that by focusing too closely on an image you could lose sight of the real person underneath.

"I'm going to get some ice cream. Do you want some?" Amy asked as she got to her feet.

"I want something calorie-free," Lila said without opening her eyes.

"Me, too," Jessica murmured.

The concession stand was crowded, and Amy took her place in line. She was just beginning to feel impatient when she heard a familiar voice behind her.

"Amy Sutton! I didn't know cheerleader-phone counselors moonlighted as beach bums!"

It was Barry.

Amy turned. "Hi! Thanks for the flowers," she said shyly.

Barry looked cute. He was wearing neon-gre[...]
swimming trunks and a pair of sunglasses hun[...]
on a cord around his neck.

Barry grinned. "Hey," he said. "What's a
friend for?"

For a moment neither said anything.

"You know," Amy said suddenly, and at the
exact same time Barry said, "I was thinking . . ."

They both broke off and laughed.

"You first," Barry said graciously.

"No, you," Amy replied.

Barry took a deep breath. "This may not be
the right time to tell you this, but I did warn
you I was a straightforward person. Amy, I've
been dying to go out with you for ages. And
when you appeared at Project Youth, I just
couldn't believe my luck. I think you're pretty
great."

Amy blushed. Barry was a little unsure of
himself, but obviously very sincere!

"Well," she said, smiling, "I just *happen* to
have some pretty terrific tickets to the Number
One concert tonight."

Barry's face lit up. "You still want to go?"

"Sure!" Amy said. Going to a concert with
Barry would be a lot of fun. She felt her spirits
lifting. So far, the weekend was turning out
to be pretty great. Dinner last night with her
parents, the beach today with her friends, and
the concert tonight with Barry!

In fact, by the time Amy returned to Jessica
and Lila, she felt as if she were floating on air.

"What's going on? You look as if you just
won the lottery," Lila said as she took the diet
soda Amy handed her.

125

rugged. "Nothing. I'm just in a good
.'s all."

, Amy, what are you going to do with
concert tickets?" Jessica asked curiously.
ju know, I wouldn't mind seeing the Num-
er One."

"Neither would I," Lila added.

"Thanks, but I'm going with Barry Rork,"
Amy said calmly as she unwrapped her ice-
cream bar.

Lila looked surprised. "You're kidding," Lila
said. "Isn't he a little, I don't know. . . ."

"Nice," Amy said firmly. "He's nice. And he
happens to be my friend."

Jessica laughed. "That's telling her, Amy!"

Amy finished unpeeling the wrapper from
her ice-cream bar and polished it off in minutes.
Come to think of it, maybe Barry was already
more than a friend. Who could tell? Lately, it
seemed as if anything could happen!

Thirteen

When Elizabeth met Enid for lunch on Monday, a frown creased her pretty face. "I can't believe it," she said. "Have you heard that the Chamber of Commerce is sponsoring a beauty pageant in Sweet Valley? They're advertising all over town for fifteen- to eighteen-year-old girls." Elizabeth shuddered. "I thought beauty pageants were a thing of the past. A bunch of girls parading around in bathing suits and evening gowns. . . ."

"Yuck," Enid agreed. "I wonder how people at school are going to react to it." She looked across the cafeteria to the table at which Claire Middleton was sitting. Claire had recently tried out for a coveted spot as quarterback for The Gladiators, Sweet Valley High's football team. A number of girls at school had rallied around her, supporting her desire to be part of a traditionally all-male sport, and since then, Claire had been known as a strong supporter of feminist rights. "Claire's going to hate it," Enid remarked.

"And she's not the only one! I just hope the pageant doesn't get very many contestants," Elizabeth said. "Beauty pageants are completely degrading."

Enid was about to comment further when Tom McKay stopped at their table. "Can I sit with you two?" he asked, his expression serious.

"Sure," Enid said.

Elizabeth looked at Tom and smiled. She hadn't seen him since their awkward meeting at the clinic, and she wondered how he had been doing since then. True to her promise, she had not shared his secret with anyone.

Tom picked up his sandwich and put it down again. "Have you heard from Jake since he's been back in San Francisco?" he asked Enid.

"He called two nights ago. He really enjoyed meeting you, Tom," Enid said.

"Yeah, well, if he said he liked meeting me, he was just being nice. I was a bit of a jerk to him."

"Listen, Jake is a very honest person," Enid objected. "If he said he liked you, he meant it. And he asked me to say hi."

Tom brightened a little. "Your cousin's a great guy. I admire him. But I . . ." Tom searched for the right words. "He told me something in confidence, and I reacted badly. I'd like a chance to tell him I'm sorry."

Enid glanced at Elizabeth. Was that "confidence" the same one Jake had shared with her?

"You know, Tom, you could always write to Jake. Or call him."

Tom fidgeted uncomfortably. "Maybe I should do that. Have you got his address?"

"It's in my locker. I'll get it for you this afternoon," Enid promised.

They talked a little longer about Jake and his visit, and then the conversation turned to schoolwork. After about ten minutes Enid excused herself. "If I don't cram for my math quiz, I'm in for it!" She waved to Elizabeth and promised to get Jake's address for Tom.

For a moment neither Elizabeth nor Tom spoke. Then he broke the silence.

"What I like the most about Jake is that he knows who he is. That sort of knowledge takes a lot of guts."

"You're not kidding," Elizabeth agreed softly.

Tom met her eyes. "I don't know yet if I'll ever be that sure of myself. But I hope I can be."

Elizabeth put her hand on his arm. "I believe you will be, Tom."

Tom's face was full of emotion. "It's good being able to talk to you, Liz. You know, I'm glad I ran into you at the clinic last week. I'm glad a couple of people know what I'm going through."

"Are you . . . have you talked to your family yet? Or to your friends?"

"I talked to Barry a little. And I'll talk to my

mom and dad someday. Right now, I'm still trying to figure out what the questions are, let alone the answers! And I'd like to have some answers when I approach them." Tom smiled.

Elizabeth looked at Tom with real warmth. His friendship and confidence meant a great deal. She felt much closer to Tom than she ever had, and she was sure they were going to become good friends. She wanted to be part of whatever it was that lay ahead for him.

"You really want to do an interview with me for the paper?" Amy Sutton asked Elizabeth incredulously.

"I really do. I want to know how you first became interested in the clinic, what sort of work you do there, how you go about solving problems. . . ." Elizabeth took out her pen and paper, ready to jot down Amy's responses.

Amy shook her head. "Wait a second. This story's going to be in *The Oracle*, for everyone at school to read, right?"

"What's wrong with that?" Elizabeth asked her. "Don't you want people to know more about the clinic? You might even attract a few more volunteers."

Amy wrapped a strand of blond hair around one finger. "That's true," she murmured. "Are you interviewing Barry, too?"

"Right after you," Elizabeth replied.

Amy smiled. It might be fun, seeing their interviews side by side. And she was full of ideas about the clinic. She had just completed her report for Ms. Jacobi and discovered her sociology grade was up to a B + !

"OK. I'll tell you about it. But I can't reveal our clients' real names, and some material is confidential," Amy said earnestly.

For the next twenty minutes Amy described exactly what a phone counselor did at the clinic, who made the calls, and the philosophy of Project Youth. "I guess what I like best about the job is that I can help people without having to be super 'professional.' Sometimes what works best is just being myself," she told Elizabeth.

Elizabeth put her pen down and smiled at Amy. "I really admire you, Amy. It sounds as if you all do a wonderful job. I'm not sure I'd have the confidence to field calls from kids who really need help."

Amy shrugged. "At first, I didn't think I did, either. But you figure things out as you go."

Like most things, Amy thought. Like learning to have more confidence in herself. Like learning she could stand on her own two feet, with or without a boyfriend.

"I'm glad you're doing the story," Amy said suddenly. She hoped that when it was published, *everyone* would read it. Including Kirk Anderson!

Last time he ever calls someone a dumb blonde, Amy thought with a chuckle. He was going to have to learn that people were not always what they seemed!

*   *   *

131

Jessica could barely control her excitement. "Have you heard about the beauty pageant, you guys?" she demanded as she joined Lila, Cara, and Amy at lunch.

Amy looked up accusingly. "Ssshh. I was just telling everyone about the concert on Saturday night. You interrupted the best part."

"What beauty pageant?" Lila asked.

"The Chamber of Commerce is sponsoring it, and supposedly there are some great prizes." Jessica's eyes were dancing. "There'll be a bathing suit competition and a talent competition!"

"God," Lila groaned. "Talent isn't the word for the drippy things those girls do. None of them are any good. It's pathetic."

"Why so negative, Li?" Jessica demanded. "I seem to remember you were pretty keen to get on Eric Parker's TV show. I thought you loved being in the spotlight." Jessica liked to remind Lila that she, Jessica, had won the coveted spot on *The Eric Parker Show.*

Lila frowned. "That wasn't a beauty contest. That was more of a talent contest. The winner had to have talent. Or she *should* have had talent," she added dryly. "Those things are always rigged."

Jessica ignored Lila's sour grapes comment. "Well, I'm going to enter the beauty pageant. I want to wear one of those banners and swoosh along the runway like the contestants on televised pageants." Jessica stood up and did a practice turn, and everyone clapped.

Amy put down her fork. "Maybe *I* should

think about competing," she said. "I always wanted to get into modeling, and if you win one of those contests, it could launch your career."

"You wouldn't really want to enter a local beauty pageant, would you?" Jessica asked. Amy would be real competition, at least as far as looks went. Of course, when it came to talent, Jessica had no doubt that she was the natural winner.

"What are you going to do for the talent competition, Jessica?" Cara asked.

Lila giggled. "How about a cheerleading routine?"

Jessica was getting annoyed. "That's not such a ridiculous idea, you know. I could do one of our special routines."

Amy rolled her eyes. "You're only saying that because you know that's what *I* want to do, Jessica."

"Well, I'll choose some other talent then." Jessica's eyes sparkled. "I'm going to enter this contest, and what's more, I'm going to win!"

"This I can't wait to see," Lila said. Cara laughed in agreement.

But Amy said nothing. She was wondering how Barry Rork would feel about her entering a beauty pageant.

"So listen," Barry said as he and Amy sat over a hamburger special that evening at the Dairi Burger. "I consider this our first real date.

You got those tickets to the concert with some-one else in mind."

Amy giggled. "How do you know the whole thing with Tom wasn't just an elaborate ruse?" she teased him.

Barry took a bite of his hamburger. "Well, that's a flattering thought." He looked at her closely. "So are you going to keep working at Project Youth?"

"I'm supposed to talk to Kathy about that tomorrow," Amy told him. "She mentioned the possibility of staying on for a while, and I'd really like to."

"Good." Barry grinned. "More time to look at those gorgeous eyes of yours."

Amy fiddled with her straw. "You know," she said casually, "Jessica was saying today at lunch that the Chamber of Commerce is spon-soring a beauty pageant in Sweet Valley. You don't think I'd have a chance of winning, do you?"

"A chance? Are you kidding? Amy, don't you have any idea of how beautiful you are?" Barry cried.

Amy smiled. That was exactly the kind of encouragement she had hoped for. "And how would you feel about a cheerleader-telephone counselor-beach bum moonlighting as a beauty pageant contestant?" she asked, only half kid-ding. Amy respected Barry a great deal. If he thought beauty pageants were awful, she had a feeling she would seriously reconsider entering.

"I'd feel just fine," Barry said. His fingers inched their way toward her. "Amy," he added seriously, "I like the fact that you're *you*. You happen to be a sensitive, thoughtful person who's also a lot of fun. And you're drop-dead beautiful. Why not enter a contest if you want to? I think it sounds like fun."

Will the beauty pageant turn out to be a dream come true—or a nightmare? Find out in Sweet Valley High #76, MISS TEEN SWEET VALLEY.

*Celebrate the Seasons
with SWEET VALLEY HIGH
Super Editions*

You've been a SWEET VALLEY HIGH fan all along—hanging out with Jessica and Elizabeth and their friends at Sweet Valley High. And now the SWEET VALLEY HIGH *Super Editions* give you more of what you like best—more romance—more excitement—more real-life adventure! Whether you're bicycling up the California Coast in PERFECT SUMMER, dancing at the Sweet Valley Christmas Ball in SPECIAL CHRISTMAS, touring the South of France in SPRING BREAK, catching the rays in a MALIBU SUMMER, or skiing the snowy slopes in WINTER CARNIVAL—you know you're exactly where you want to be—with the gang from SWEET VALLEY HIGH.

SWEET VALLEY HIGH SUPER EDITIONS

☐ **PERFECT SUMMER**
25072/$2.95

☐ **SPRING BREAK**
25537/$2.95

☐ **SPECIAL CHRISTMAS**
25377/$2.95

☐ **MALIBU SUMMER**
26050/$2.95

☐ **WINTER CARNIVAL**
26159/$2.95

☐ **SPRING FEVER**
26420/$2.95

Series
Don't miss any of the Caitlin trilogies
Created by Francine Pascal

There has never been a heroine quite like the raven-haired, unforgettable beauty, Caitlin. Dazzling, charming, rich, and very, very clever Caitlin Ryan seems to have everything. Everything, that is, but the promise of lasting love. The three trilogies follow Caitlin from her family life at Ryan Acres, to Highgate Academy, the exclusive boarding school in the posh horse country of Virginia, through college, and on to a glamorous career in journalism in New York City.

Don't miss Caitlin!

THE LOVE TRILOGY

☐	27650	AGAINST THE ODDS #51	$2.95
☐	27720	WHITE LIES #52	$2.95
☐	27771	SECOND CHANCE #53	$2.95
☐	27856	TWO BOY WEEKEND #54	$2.95
☐	27915	PERFECT SHOT #55	$2.95
☐	27970	LOST AT SEA #56	$2.95
☐	28079	TEACHER CRUSH #57	$2.95
☐	28156	BROKEN HEARTS #58	$2.95
☐	28193	IN LOVE AGAIN #59	$2.95
☐	28264	THAT FATAL NIGHT #60	$2.95
☐	28317	BOY TROUBLE #61	$2.95
☐	28352	WHO'S WHO #62	$2.95
☐	28385	THE NEW ELIZABETH #63	$2.95
☐	28487	THE GHOST OF TRICIA MARTIN #64	$2.95
☐	28518	TROUBLE AT HOME #65	$2.95
☐	28555	WHO'S TO BLAME #66	$2.95
☐	28611	THE PARENT PLOT #67	$2.95
☐	28618	THE LOVE BET #68	$2.95
☐	28636	FRIEND AGAINST FRIEND #69	$2.95
☐	28767	MS. QUARTERBACK #70	$2.95
☐	28796	STARRING JESSICA #71	$2.95
☐	28841	ROCK STAR'S GIRL #72	$2.95
☐	28863	REGINA'S LEGACY #73	$2.95

__ Buy them at your local bookstore or use this page to order. __

Bantam Books, Dept. SVH7, 414 East Golf Road, Des Plaines, IL 60016

Please send me the items I have checked above. I am enclosing $_____
(please add $2.50 to cover postage and handling). Send check or money
order, no cash or C.O.D.s please.

Mr/Ms _____

Address _____

City/State _____ Zip _____

SVH7—4/91

Please allow four to six weeks for delivery.
Prices and availability subject to change without notice.